CHERRINGHAM

A COSY MYSTERY SERIES

MURDER ON THAMES

Neil Richards • Matthew Costello

RED DOG
UK

Published by RED DOG PRESS 2020

Originally published as an eBook edition by Bastei Lübbe AG,
Cologne, Germany, 2013.

ISBN 978-1-913331-54-2

www.reddogpress.co.uk

Cherringham is a long-running mystery series set in the Cotswolds. The stories are self-contained, though many will enjoy reading them in order of publication:

Murder on Thames
Mystery at the Manor
Murder by Moonlight
Thick as Thieves
Last Train to London
The Curse of Mabb's Farm
The Body in the Lake
Snowblind
Playing Dead
A Deadly Confession
Blade in the Water
Death on a Summer Night

MURDER ON THAMES

1.

A BRISK WALK.

MRS LOUELLA TIDEWELL — just 'Lou' to her friends — pulled up the collar of her coat as the breeze off the river swept right through her. Brady, her Black Labrador, raced through the open meadow, somehow — Lou hoped — dodging all the horse manure.

Labs, she thought, not for the first time, are so smart.

And what good company Brady had made since Mr Tidewell passed away: one minute reading his paper, a glass of sherry at his side, and the next, eyes shut — gone.

Leaving Lou alone. She might have lots of friends, but it wasn't quite the same, was it?

Now she kept walking, letting herself drift closer to the river that passed near the village, beautiful on a sunny summer's day, but now so dark and grey that it seemed almost ominous on this overcast morning.

"Don't think we'll see the sun today," she said.

She didn't mind speaking to herself when she was alone. She might have told herself, as she did at home, that she was talking to Brady.

Turning to him she saw that the dog had stopped dead in his

tracks, as though he had spied a stray rabbit and reverted to some ancient memory of a past life as a hunting dog.

It was almost as if he was pointing towards the long bend in the river where it widened. A weir had been built, but next to it the river channel still flowed fast, especially when it rained heavily. And these days, Lou thought to herself, we certainly seem to get our share of horrible downpours.

"What is it, boy? Seen something to chase?"

But instead of racing over to investigate, Brady ran back and circled her legs. Another breeze hit her and she brought her hand up to check that her coat was buttoned up at the neck.

Brady whimpered.

Odd, she thought. He only really did that when he wanted to get out for his walk, to tend to business.

Suddenly Brady leaped away again, just a few feet, as if encouraging her to follow. She really would have liked to turn back home, get inside where it was warm. A nice cup of English Breakfast tea and a toasted slice of multigrain from Huffington's, the local bakery-cum-coffee shop. She'd smear it in marmalade and — why not? — butter. Read the paper.

Yes, that's what she wanted to do.

Instead, with Brady acting pretty peculiar, she started walking in the direction he seemed to want her to go, the Lab leading the way with an eagerness that Lou didn't feel.

She had to watch her step — and not just because of the droppings. Off the main path that followed the river the land looked flat but was, in reality, filled with ruts and depressions, all hidden by the thick foot-high grass blowing in the early morning wind.

"Easy, Brady," she said to the barking dog. "I'm coming, just need to take care."

She took a breath, the morning chill clinging to her lungs.

Now Brady charged ahead. They were close to where the river forked, one side wandering to the weir, the other meandering its way down to the other villages that it lazily rolled by.

The mighty Thames, here but a sleepy river.

Brady had stopped. Once again, he had turned to stone. Standing stock-still, and looking across to the weir, his gaze was focused directly on the shallow waters where the stream frothed and bubbled.

She came abreast of her dog, reached down and gave his head a slow stroke.

"Don't know what you see, boy. Maybe there are rabbits over there, on the other side, but—"

She stopped.

At first it was one of those moments, happening more now with age, where you see something and you say,' "Oh, that's a…"

And you guess it's *this*, then, as you look closer, take a step nearer, you make another guess.

She did that now and saw what looked like a bit of cloth; shiny, sparkly, festive, glimmering even in this dull morning light, competing with the shimmering river water.

She moved closer and realized that she was looking at clothes.

A skirt of some kind. And something dull but still white. A blouse.

Her mind quickly filled in the details; perhaps a part of her even knew before she actually acknowledged it, what exactly she was looking at.

An area of muddy brown turned out to be a bowed head, chin to chest, face and eyes hidden.

And as that became clear, Lou slowly started to make sense of what she could see: arms poking out of a blouse, one horizontal to the body, fingers lazily pointing east, the other dangling in the rushing water, its hand hidden.

"Dear sweet God," Lou said to herself.

Brady had been whimpering but at the sound of her voice turned to look at her. To Lou it seemed as though his eyes were sad, as if he knew this was wrong.

And though normally she would let her dog just bounce and gambol his way back to the village, racing to her small cottage just outside the main square, now she dug the leash out of her pocket and clipped it to Brady's worn collar.

She wanted him beside her, even if he tugged and pulled as she made her way back to the village, to the police, to tell them what she had seen.

2.
SARAH AND SAMMI

SARAH TURNED OFF the TV.

"All right you lot, now you're late. Grab your bags, and lunches — fast — and let's move."

As she piled the cereal bowls in the sink, Sarah watched her two children, Chloe, thirteen, and Daniel, ten, drift slowly out towards the hall. Though they didn't complain much about school, they certainly didn't radiate eagerness in the morning.

And Chloe seemed to grow more secretive and quieter by the day.

Reminds me of me, Sarah thought. *What a handful I was.* She did a quick scan of the kitchen to make sure everything electric was off. Only a few weeks ago some little old lady in one of the sheltered flats at the far end of the village had let a toaster turn her flat into... toast.

She'd got into the habit of double-checking everything. *After all, look what happened to my lovely marriage. One minute a happy couple then all the cheating comes out, and suddenly here we are. A stereotype. Two kids. Single mum, of a certain age — whatever that was supposed to mean.* The children started trudging out of the little semi to the Rav4, one of the few things she was able to salvage from the wreck of her London life.

"You can have the car. And the remaining twelve payments," Oliver had said with a grin. *Bastard.*

She pulled the front door tight and stepped over Chloe and Daniel's bikes. God, that lawn needed mowing. It was only a tiny patch, but somehow it was like a meadow. She couldn't do it today though busy day ahead — three good web pitches to sort.

She liked to keep as busy as possible and it seemed lately, between the children and the studio, she had nothing to worry about on that score.

AFTER DROPPING OFF Chloe she stopped at Cherringham Primary. At 8.30 on a weekday morning the stretch of road outside the school turned into a Grand Prix pit-stop. Mums and dads thronged at the main gate, prams and buggies jostled, cars weaved in and out dropping off children in record time before shooting off down the road.

As usual there was nowhere to park, so she stopped in the middle of the road and waited while Daniel climbed out the back.

"Got swimming tonight, mum, so I'll be late."

"All right love, see you at home," said Sarah, waiting for the door to slam. But before she could pull away, a face leaned in through her open window — the dreaded Angela.

"Shocking, isn't it?" said Angela, her chubby cheeks pink with the effort of holding a dribbling toddler high on her shoulder.

"Hmm? What?" Sarah said absently. Angela served as the key hub in the village gossip machine and very little escaped her notice — or her condemnation. Sarah waited politely for today's instalment to be completed.

She wasn't prepared for what Angela said next.

"And you… you must be *so* upset. What with her being your best mate and all."

Suddenly, Angela's words cut through the morning air,

matching the chilling wind as the woman hovered by the window.

"What are you talking about, Angela?" Sarah asked impatiently.

"Sammi Charlton, of course," said Angela. "I just assumed someone would have told you. They reckon it was an overdose. Wouldn't surprise me, she used to do all sorts of things, didn't she? Not that I'm saying you did too, of course."

"Angela." Sarah kept her voice steady. She and Sammi had been such good friends. But that was long ago; before London, before Sammi vanished. "What's happened to Sammi?" said Sarah, dreading the answer.

"Oh, they found her down in the weir this morning. Drowned. Thought for sure someone would have told..." Angela tailed off.

Sarah felt her stomach turn. Sammi dead.

For all of her friend's craziness, that seemed unreal. And not just dead, but dead *here*, after so many years away, back in the village where they had both grown up.

"Are you sure?"

A car behind Sarah hooted impatiently. Angela began to turn away before giving her final judgement on the matter.

"Oh yes, dear. No doubt about it. Dead as they come."

SARAH PARKED IN the square and picked up a coffee from Huffington's before heading to the studio. The ground floor estate agents didn't open till ten and she was usually first into the building.

Picking up the post, she climbed the flights of narrow stairs to the top floor, where she turned on the computers on her desk and went over to the window.

From here, three floors up, she could see down into the village square and also across the rooftops to the river and the far meadows.

There wasn't a lot of room but with a view like that, she loved her office.

From up here the weir was hidden by dense trees. But she could see that the traffic heading to the toll bridge was slow-moving, crawling. The police must still be down there.

A body found in their quiet little village. She sipped the coffee, so hot.

She still couldn't believe it. Sammi — dead?

Sammi had been her mate all right. But that word couldn't possibly convey what she and Sammi had meant to each other.

Sammi had been her true pal, her best friend, her shoulder to cry on, her partner—in-crime all through their teen years, through GCSEs and A-levels. They had laughed, danced, played and drunk together during the most intense (and possibly the best) part of their lives.

One year they even shared boyfriends — God what a mess that had been. Although later they had managed to laugh about it as they compared notes.

And then — funny how it always happens — they'd just got used to not seeing each other much, each picking a different path.

Sammi went off to drama school while Sarah went to university. Sammi went around the world chasing her dream of being an actor, while Sarah moved to London, got a job, married Oliver and had children.

But slowly Sarah started to see warning signs that all was not well.

Every once in a while, Sammi would turn up unannounced needing a bed for the night and, after a prickly start, the two of them would open a bottle of wine, then another and another — they'd reminisce and Sammi would talk till dawn about her hair-raising adventures. Then she would go off to the airport and Sarah wouldn't see her again — till next time.

The last time she had seen Sammi had been two years ago in London — when she and Oliver were still together. Sammi was apparently modeling in Tokyo — though it all sounded dodgy to Sarah. This time, with the children in bed, the three of them had stayed up drinking too much. As the evening wore on Sammi turned flirty with Oliver; too flirty for Sarah's liking.

But Oliver — another early warning sign — hadn't seemed to mind.

There'd been a massive row and everyone had gone to bed angry. Sammi had left for the airport at dawn without saying goodbye, and Sarah hadn't seen her since. Nor ever would again, she realized.

She looked down at the village square — at the tea-rooms, the café. The bus shelter. The old pub — the Angel. The stone bench outside the village hall. The library with its big porch. Once upon a time she and Sammi had *owned* that square. It had been *their* patch. Every square inch of it.

Sarah wiped her eyes, sat at her desk, logged on and started to work. Things happen — she knew that all too well. She had three website design pitches to finish today and she didn't have time for memories.

At least, not yet.

3.

THE CAUSE OF DEATH

"YOU STAY THERE, Riley," said Jack Brennan, as he closed the shutters on the cabin doors and clicked the padlock carefully shut.

Riley stood waiting on the river bank, tail wagging, desperate to be unleashed into the nice summer morning and the delights of the meadow. Jack pocketed the key and stepped across the planks that linked his boat, which he'd christened 'The Grey Goose', to dry land.

Out of habit, he checked the mooring lines fore and aft and gave the big old Dutch barge a once-over along the waterline. Soon be time for another lick of paint, he thought to himself.

He was looking forward to it. He liked to be occupied.

Checking he had Riley's lead in his pocket, he set off down the towpath for their morning walk.

THREE MILES THERE and back: Jack Brennan had made this trip every morning, come rain, snow or shine, ever since he had arrived here from New York.

One and a half hours it took, including the coffee and free read of the paper up at the weird little cafe in the village. Time was he'd have run the miles but these days he valued his knees and was aiming to get another thirty years out of them, so walking was just fine.

Riley ran ahead, though never more than a hundred yards. The Springer knew the score: he and Jack had spent an interesting summer when Riley was just a puppy working out the terms of their relationship and now they had it down to a tee. Riley had finally agreed with all of Jack's rules — though he'd taken some persuading.

A tad wilful, not unlike his owner. Maybe more than a tad.

Jack breathed in deep. Today was just the kind of day that told him he'd made the right decision to come and live here. Though the morning had been quite cold and wet, the sun had come out and it was warming up already. On the other side of the river, a heat haze hung over the meadow and just overhead, the swallows dived and swooped.

It was a very long way from the gulls and fishing boats of Bay Ridge, New York.

Along the river all the residential boats were just coming alive with the sound of TVs, radios and the smell of bacon and eggs.

There were boats every twenty yards or so — a real hotchpotch of canal barges, river cruisers, yachts, little day-boats, speedboats. So English, this odd community.

But then, what would you expect at the cheaper end of the village? Further downstream, on the other side of Cherringham Toll Bridge, the big plastic gin-palaces were moored, boats big enough to host cocktail parties and outdoor dinners.

Jack guessed a good amount of London money found its way down here.

Not that he ever got invited. Jack Brennan was not the right sort. American, living on an old barge, daily shaving no longer mandatory. He had gotten used to the locals looking him up and down. Just a quick smile back, and they moved on, probably wondering... What's a Yank doing living here... and on the river no less?

As he reached a curve in the bank, Cherringham came into view up on the far hill and Jack could just hear the church bells ringing.

Tuesday, Bell Ringing Practice day, he thought. With a bit of luck they'd have stopped by the time he ordered his macchiato — much as he liked a bit of local colour, church bells had a time and a place, and during his breakfast wasn't it.

As he rounded the curve, Jack caught sight of something that jarred with the peaceful surroundings.

It was something that Jack had once known well, though not here, on his new home turf.

Up ahead by the weir sat an ambulance and two police cars, lights flashing. Nearby, there was a white truck, men scrambling out in matching white suits.

Jack guessed that they were crime scene investigators, though this British version looked more like a hazmat team.

They sure do things differently around here, he thought.

And that was a main reason he wanted to come this far. To get away. Far away. From a lot of things...

Police had surrounded the weir area with black-and-yellow tape, while up on the bridge a handful of locals stood watching the show.

"Riley!" he called. Riley came back reluctantly and Jack clipped on the short lead. His dog may be curious and headstrong — but he always came back on a dime.

As he approached the tape a young policeman stepped up, blocking the river path.

"Sorry, sir, we've had an incident here. 'Fraid, you'll have to go round across the fields," he said.

"No problem," said Jack.

The policeman looked at him a little more closely. The accent.

"Don't get a lot of Americans here."

Jack felt an unfamiliar ripple. Suspicion.

"Live on one of the boats, do you sir?"

Jack nodded. "That I do."

"So — you'll know the way round then," the cop replied.

Jack nodded again, and turned to go.

"Come on, Riley," he said.

Jack wasn't interested in the crime scene. That was one thing he'd had his fill of back in the States. Whatever had happened here would be just fine without him knowing a single damn thing about it.

But as he took the long way round, he could sense the cop's eyes on him. Funny — if you didn't stick your nose in things round here, people straight away thought there was something odd about you.

Even after a year in England, this place could still baffle him.

SARAH TURNED OFF her computer.

What a day. She'd finished two of the three design pitches, but she hadn't been able to face the third. A new website for Bassett and Son's Funeral Directors and right now Sarah wished she'd told both Bassett and his son where to go: one of them wanted "something upbeat and cheerful" and the other wanted "respectful and solemn."

She'd give them respect...

She checked the time. Six o'clock. The kids would both be late back from school and they wouldn't be expecting tea till seven.

She grabbed her car keys and headed out.

DOWN BY THE RIVER, the traffic now flowed freely. Sarah parked on the village side of the toll bridge and walked across before heading down into the little car park where one police car was still parked.

Further upriver she could see the weir, and another police car.

She headed up the river path, still warm in the setting sun. The scent of jasmine seemed incongruous: she was walking to the scene of her best friend's death, not out for a stroll in the country.

She had debated not doing this. Somehow, though, coming here seemed right.

The police had put up tape all around the weir area, but now she watched the solitary policeman on duty taking it down.

She knew him. How many times had he asked her out since she came back to the village? And when would he stop?

"Hello Alan," she called as she approached.

The policeman turned, the tape in great loops round his arms.

"Was going to stop by, you know. Thought with it being Sammi and all, you'd be well, upset."

"So what happened?"

"Sarah. You know I can't tell you that. And we're still investigating. But you know Sammi."

"*Knew*. Come on Alan," she said

"There's procedure I got to follow, rules and that."

"For God's sake," she said. "You, me and Sammi, we used to drink Scrumpy down here together. You want me to remind everyone how you and she got caught skinny-dipping that time?"

He smiled. "You think I don't remember that?" he said. "Just because I got this uniform on, don't mean it's easy for me either, okay?"

Sarah softened.

"Yeah, I know."

"This — this is a lot of crap, this is, being down here on my own."

Sarah put her hand on his shoulder hoping it would not be misinterpreted.

"I'm sorry, Alan."

He nodded — clearly glad of the comfort.

"We had good times, didn't we?" he said.

"Yeah, we did. Never quite knew what she'd do next, our Sammi."

Alan laughed.

"Stuck her fingers up at old Cherringham didn't she," he said. "London. The high life. Don't blame her sometimes."

Sarah nodded.

"So okay. What did happen?"

Alan shrugged. He took a step closer to her. The warmth of the summer day had finally started to fade.

"All right. But listen, you didn't hear it from me, okay? Some old dear found her this morning. She was caught up in the weir, stuck there, half underwater. The crime scene team reckon she fell in upriver and floated down, got snagged up here like."

"Did you know she had come back to Cherringham?"

"Nope. Though I heard she turned up at the Ploughman last night, so they say. Had a few."

"Few too many, you think?"

Knowing Sammi, it could have been things other than pints and shots. She had embraced that part of the high life as well.

"I reckon. You ask me, she comes down here, has a smoke. Always one for the wacky backy wasn't she? Has too much, goes along the river bank, falls in. Or maybe she tries to have a swim. Crazy girl."

"Where have they taken her?"

"Her body? Gone to Swindon in a bag," he said. "They'll do the post-mortem there." He sniffed the air. The Sherlock Holmes of

Cherringham. "My guess -- it will be accidental drowning."

Sarah looked at Alan and for a brief second saw in his face the teenager she'd known at school.

"I'm going to walk along the path. Upriver. That okay?"

"Yeah. Sure. Guess you got your own thoughts, memories to sort... This place is open now anyway. Just — stay away from the edge, eh?"

He wasn't smiling.

"I will," she said.

She nodded at him and walked away thinking that yes this might be about memories and all that. But maybe it was something more. Sammi drowning? Falling in the chilly river?

Something about that made no sense at all.

4.

JACK AND SARAH

JACK LEANED BACK into his deckchair and puffed gently on a Cohiba — a real Havana — and watched the sun drift gently down behind the distant village.

These moments, on warm summer evenings like this, were perfection.

Ahead of him the Thames flowed, still deep and broad enough to attract little cruisers, kayaks and rowing boats out for an evening spin.

At his side on the warm wooden deck, Riley snoozed, as if he knew he was off duty. And on the other side, on the little card table, was a vodka martini, the clear liquid catching the light of the setting sun.

The silvery shaker sweated on the table next to it,

Back at Marty's Bar in Sheepshead Bay, Jack would tell the owner how to make the perfect martini. For Marty, the "bat and ball" of a shot and beer chaser was about as complicated as it got.

Katherine had loved her martini as well. All the way until the very end.

He took a sip. *To Katherine,* he thought.

On his lap sat the little box of floaters, twine, feathers and hair from which he was about to make his first ever fishing lure. He might be over fifty but there were still things he was learning, and fly-fishing was one of them.

He breathed out, satisfied. Perfection? Maybe, if he hadn't been alone, though he swore to himself that he had to stop thinking about the past and the future he had lost.

And every day it got easier.

"Excuse me!"

The voice was loud — louder than it needed to be on a quiet evening like this — and somehow impatient. Riley stood up, ears perked, to see what the fuss was.

Jack turned awkwardly in his deckchair to look at the river bank. A woman stood by his gangplank watching him. She was in her late thirties, medium height — about five-seven — maybe a hundred-forty pounds, slim, blue eyes, blonde spiky hair — kind of an elfin cut.

White blouse, long blue shorts, trainers. In good shape, a runner, maybe, from the look of her legs and waist. Professional, business-like.

You can stop working as a detective, but you will always be one, he thought. Still liked to get the details straight. Every picture — and every profile — tells a story.

"Can I come aboard?"

Jack considered this.

"No. Sorry."

The woman looked taken aback — as if he'd just insulted her.

"Oh. I see."

Jack watched her as she considered her next approach. Since he had never signed up to any of the English rituals of politeness, antiquated manners and codes of behaviour, he had kind of got used to this reaction.

"I'm terribly sorry" she said. "What I mean is — do you have a moment?"

"How can I help you?" He took a puff on the cigar, its silvery ash growing.

"See… something happened, on the river. Maybe you saw all the police, and I wondered if you were on your boat last night?"

"I might have been." He forced a smile. "You doing some undercover work, officer?"

She smiled back at that, and brushed at her hair. "No. Sorry. It's just, I wondered if you heard anything?"

Jack thought for a minute.

"No. Now, if you don't mind, miss—"

"I mean — heard anything unusual. You know?"

"I did say, 'No'."

"So you didn't hear anything at all?"

"The answer's still the same — no."

"You see, the thing is, a friend of mine — well, the police say she fell in the river and drowned, you see, in the night, just down there."

"Uh-huh. I saw the police lights. And — to be honest — wasn't terribly interested."

Another puff, followed by a last sip of his martini. Time for another.

"In the weir. Someone found her, caught there. Dead. Just this morning. My friend Sammi. So anyway, I was walking along here, thinking that if she fell in it might have been up here somewhere. So that's why I wondered if maybe you heard something in the night?"

The woman smiled as if that might make him more interested in helping her. He almost felt sorry for her. How could she know he was done with all of that?

Totally done.

"No. Not a thing."

The woman frowned, and chewed her lower lip.

She was obviously disappointed — but there wasn't anything he could do about it. And anyway, the last thing he wanted right now was a conversation about some poor girl who had fallen into the river and drowned. He wanted to get back to making his fly and watching his sunset, which was almost over.

But the woman lingered.

Persistent indeed. Then:

"Fine," she said. "Okay. And thanks for your help."

Persistent *and* sarcastic. "No problem."

She took a step away then stopped, and turned. "Oh I can see that. Not a problem — for *you*. Anyway, if you happen to remember anything perhaps you could tell the police? That would be very … good of you. Think you could do that?"

"Sure. I'll remember that."

She started to walk away, and Jack swore he could hear, so faintly, *bloody Yank*.

Haven't done much to improve our "special friends" view of Americans.

Riley watched her go, then came back to Jack's side and lay down again.

Jack settled back in his deckchair. He picked up the shaker, poured, and took a long sip of now melted ice water, then stared at the deep, flowing water of the Thames as it slid by his boat.

Then he took up the little roll of twine and a tiny red feather, and started to lay out the hooks on the card table.

So they reckoned the body had fallen in the river up here? And suddenly he wasn't thinking about the fly, the cigar, or even the sun slipping below the horizon.

Well that didn't make any sense. No sense at all.

5.

THE DAY AFTER

SARAH STARED AT the artwork from the Bassett and Son Funeral Directors marketing manager and shut her eyes. Was this really what her life had become? This time three years ago she would have been wowing clients in Cannes with her ideas on kickass social media campaigning.

Now it was 'Buy One Funeral, Get One Free'. Was she really going to have to explain why that worked with pizzas but maybe not with Death?

And God, did her head hurt.

The kids had burned their tea last night, setting off the fire alarm. In the fuss she'd forgotten to eat. Then she'd drunk a whole bottle of red wine on her own — memories of Sammi swirling — and fallen asleep on the sofa in front of a stupid chick flick that she always watched and always hated.

Grace put a coffee on her desk and smiled.

"Oh, bless you. What would I do without you, Grace?"

"You'd probably make a profit — a tiny one -- but I'm not complaining."

Sarah laughed. Grace was a total find — eighteen, hard-working, smart and ambitious. Oh, to be eighteen again.

Sarah put her head on her arms on the desk. Maybe a power nap would help. The phone rang — Grace picked it up and put it through to Sarah's extension.

"Some guy for you. Says it's important."

Sarah mimed — *who is it?*

"Dunno. Sounds American, I think."

Sarah frowned. There was only one American she'd talked to recently and she didn't want to spend another second in his company. Surely it wasn't him.

She picked up the phone.

"Sarah Edwards."

The voice on the other end didn't miss a beat.

"Your friend Sammi. Been thinking. This notion she fell in upriver. That your idea — or the police?"

Sarah didn't have time to think, let alone be annoyed. The American from the boat — what was this about?

"It's what the police say. The evidence, I guess."

"Well the police are wrong. You want to know what really happened to her?"

"I don't know what you mean," said Sarah.

"I can't really say it clearer. Do you want to know how your friend Sammi died?"

What had happened to the hostile Yank?

"Yes. Yes, of course."

"Good, because I doubt that she fell in."

"That's what I was thinking as well."

"Ok — free now? I'll see you at the weir in ten."

"But…" The line went dead. Sarah stared into space, then picked up her handbag and phone.

"Grace — I'm going out for a bit." Then on impulse she added, "And if I don't come back — tell the police I went to see that American living down on the river. Okay?"

"The American? What's happening Sarah?"

But Sarah had gone.

SHE PARKED THE car in the weir car park.

The police tape had gone. Nobody would ever guess that a body had been pulled out of the frothing water just twenty-four hours earlier. Village life and the villagers all ready to move on, nice and tidy.

She looked up at the sound of an outboard motor. A boat was approaching — and in it sat the rude American she'd had the misfortune of meeting the day before. Sitting next to him was his brown Springer Spaniel.

At least the dog looked friendly.

The tall American looked almost comical in the little boat. Deeply tanned, in a faded white polo shirt and jeans, he had a confident, self-contained look, as if he truly didn't care what the world thought of him.

His salt-and-pepper hair was tousled, like a boy who's not seen a mirror for a whole summer. The stubble on his face from the night before had vanished.

And as the boat got closer, she could see that the jeans — though faded — were pressed.

He nodded to her, and cut the outboard, easing the boat against the jetty. He threw up a rope up — surprising her — but she caught it and wrapped it once round a bollard.

"Hop in," he said, looking up at her. "Riley — make some space there."

The dog shuffled up to the bow of the little boat. Sarah stayed where she was.

"What's up — you scared of the water?" he said. "Or is it the boat?"

"It's not the boat I'm worried about. It's *you*. Were you a boatman back in the States?"

"Boatman?" He laughed. "It's okay. I know what I'm doing. More or less. Done a lot of fishing off Breezy in my day."

"Breezy? Wherever the hell that is. So — you want me to get in your boat when I don't even know your name?"

"Jack Brennan."

"And you are here to…? You could be anybody. The friendly local serial killer — you name it."

"Well, I'm not. I used to be a cop, a NYPD detective actually. If you're nice hey I'll even show you the badge. I got awards, citations — all that jazz. You can check me out. But right now, I want to show you something important about your pal Sammi."

"Why?"

"Because I hate it when cops get the basics wrong." He sniffed the air. "And they sometimes do."

"And you think they've got this wrong?"

"Oh yes. Very wrong. Hop in — and I'll show you."

Jack held the boat steady and stared at her expectantly.

Sarah had a fleeting thought that this moment was going to change her life. Then the thought was gone.

She took his outstretched hand and climbed aboard next to the American's dog.

JACK FLICKED THE line free, fired up the outboard, and then spun the boat round and headed away from the quay.

Sarah sat with Riley in the bow facing Jack as he steered the boat up river. She didn't take her eyes off him.

He smiled to himself.

"Relax. Please?"

"So how did you get my number? In fact, how did you know my name?"

"Like I said — I used to be a cop."

"Right. I will check on that."

She went silent. Jack steered the boat past lines of moored houseboats, slowing as they neared the Grey Goose.

"So come on," she said. "How did you find out my name, number? I'm just curious…"

He grinned at this. "Tell me, if you wanted to find out anything in this village — where would you go?"

"Huffington's."

"Correct," he said. "It's how the world survived before Google. Coffee shops and bars. Now — you see the log down there by your feet? Pick it up, would you."

Jack watched as she tugged a heavy, wet piece of old timber out from under the bench seat. She was strong, he thought to himself. A woman used to doing things for herself. That and the lack of a ring suggested there was no Mr Edwards on the scene. "Now what?" she said.

He turned the boat round, edged it into the side by the moored boats and killed the throttle. The boat bobbed slowly downstream.

"Drop the log overboard, would you?"

She heaved it over. It splashed into the river and began to drift away ahead of them.

"So," he said. "Imagine that's your friend Sammi. She's fallen in the river. It's the middle of the night. Nobody can hear her struggling."

"Thanks for making it so real."

Jack tweaked the throttle so they stayed alongside the log.

"See how she's drifting fast?"

Sarah nodded.

"Once you start to hit these bends, the river picks up speed," he said.

Jack could see that Sarah was watching the log intently now.

"See the weir coming up?"

Sarah nodded.

Jack opened the throttle, staying just alongside the log as it picked up speed.

The river was beginning to broaden. A couple of hundred yards ahead, on one side, the weir could be seen, bubbling and white, the water shallow and rocky. Beyond it and round the curve stood the outline of the old Cherringham Toll Bridge.

"Now — here you go -- watch what happens," said Jack.

The log looked as though it was going to drift straight into the weir.

But with just twenty yards to go, it suddenly veered right, picked up speed and swept past the weir into deep water.

Jack turned the boat round fast so as not to follow the log, pushed the throttle and headed for the bank and the jetty. The log now disappeared from sight, moving downriver.

"See?" he said.

Sarah turned and stared at him.

"Years ago when they made the weir, they dug a deep channel next to it. Any rubbish that comes downriver goes straight down the channel. That's why the weir's always clean. No brush, no branches… and no bodies."

"So Sammi didn't fall in upriver?" said Sarah.

"Nope. My guess is she drowned in the shallow water where she was found, right there."

"But why would anybody go walking in there?"

"Why indeed. And that's not the only thing. You see the river bank there, by the edge of the weir?"

He pointed to the muddy edge below the car park and jetty.

"There are tyre marks there. Looking fresh, not more than a day old."

"Someone brought a car down there?"

"Yup. Someone backed a vehicle down onto the weir. And then had a lot of trouble getting it out again. All that wet mud, tyres grinding in deeper." He took a breath. "Had to be a nerve-racking moment. Strange — the police must have noticed that."

"Hang on! What are you saying? Are you telling me Sammi was murdered? Someone in that car?"

Jack spoke carefully.

"I can tell you that it wasn't an accident. I've pulled enough bodies from Manhattan's waterways to know that. And if it was murder, we're going to need a whole lot of things…"

"We? And things like what?"

"Suspects. Motives. Evidence."

He looked right at her. "Your friendly local constabulary may have moved on. But now that you have, let's say, piqued my interest, you, me… we don't have a lot to move on."

And then it hit her.

Sarah realized he was talking about the two of them — together — solving what Jack said had been the murder of Sammi.

They'd do it together. And she didn't feel afraid of that idea. No, her friend deserved it, and she also had the thought—

This could be exciting.

MURDER ON THAMES

6.

QUESTIONS FOR THE POLICE

AND JUST LIKE that, they fell into making a plan. Sarah found herself caught up in what Jack explained and the way he cut through the clearly incorrect conclusions of the local police.

Now that she knew Sammi had not jumped into the river — drunk, drugged up — Sarah felt she owed one thing to her long-lost soul of a friend.

To find out who did it.

And Jack had made it clear that despite his expertise, as an outsider he'd need help — a lot of it — navigating the inner workings of an English village and the authorities who wanted things kept nice and peaceful, and who wanted any unpleasantness dealt with quickly, maybe even swept under the carpet.

They had a plausible explanation of Sammi's death so unless the post-mortem showed otherwise, this was case closed.

Except now Sarah knew it *wasn't* closed, and wouldn't be until she found out the truth.

But where to start?

Jack suggested that the local police would be a good place. They agreed to meet outside the police station just after lunch. That would mean — most likely — seeing Alan. Could be a bit awkward, having both been friends with Sammi.

But, somehow, she'd get through that.

For the moment, she decided not to tell Grace what she was up to. *Got a meeting*, she called out as she left the office.

Hurrying out into the village square, she saw that the sunny morning had given way to some early afternoon clouds.

How appropriate, she thought.

JACK STOOD OUTSIDE the police station, dressed in khakis and a tan shirt, hoping he blended in.

As he watched the locals walk down the street, he decided that maybe his look was a bit too rustic. It might fly in some Midwestern farm town but here people looked as if even a trip to the butcher's required a bit of dressing up.

It had turned chilly too. This English weather took some getting used to. One minute sunny and warm, the next, cloudy and cool. Like being on an ocean liner ploughing through the North Atlantic, which, he guessed, was sort of what this island country was actually like: sitting out in the ocean as the clouds and sun played tag with it.

He looked at his watch, waiting for Sarah, thinking… *do I really want to do this? Get involved with this mess?*

Murder or not, was it any of his business? What happened to his plans to make his flies, pull in the occasional fish? Enjoy those sunsets when granted by the gods of what they called an "English summer"'.

But years of dealing with dead people, from the innocent to those who deserved it, left Jack with the clear conviction that whoever did it *had* to be found.

Most of the time he had succeeded. A few times he hadn't, and those never left his mind.

The unsolved murders haunted him. And if he did nothing here, the same thing would happen... And now that he knew it wasn't a drowning, he couldn't let it go. This Sammi, just a young girl found dead in a river, had become important to him.

"Hello. Sorry, had a few things to clear up."

Jack turned as Sarah walked up behind him.

A smile. "No problem. Been taking in the village scene."

"Pretty exciting," she said.

"To me, yes. It's not Times Square."

"New York City. I used to love it. Back in the day."

"Yeah. It is something. So — ready to go in? Make introductions?"

She nodded, and he sensed that she didn't seem all that sure about this. "Might be a bit awkward. Asking questions and all."

"I can handle 'awkward'."

Anther nod, and she led the way into the station.

AND AS IF he'd been expecting them, Alan stood by the front desk, a sheaf of papers in his hand.

Jack stayed a few steps behind her.

"Alan."

He turned. "Sarah?" He took in Jack standing near her, looking around the station.

"Alan, this is Jack Brennan, he's—"

The policeman took a step closer, lowering the papers. "I know. You're the Yank living on that old fishing tub."

Jack nodded. A few seconds of quiet. Then:

"Alan, is there someplace we could talk? Jack here, well... he has some ideas. About Sammi. About what happened."

"You mean about the drowning?"

Sarah didn't answer. Instead: "Your office. For a bit? We had some questions."

She sensed Alan stiffen. This was not going well at all. "Questions. Well, you know, usually we ask the questions." He took a breath and seemed to relent. "All right then. But let's make it fast. Got a ton of paperwork to finish."

Another pause.

"Because of the drowning." At that he led the way past the front desk, and down a narrow hallway.

"SO, WHAT IS IT you Americans say? 'Shoot'?"

Jack heard the policeman attempt to affect an American accent, something probably culled from too many CSI episodes.

"Sarah says you have questions?"

Jack quickly picked up on the idea that these two had some history. Something in the past that wasn't there now.

He began to explain how Sarah got him involved, then about the experiment on the river, the tyre marks and how it called into question the 'official' story the police had settled at.

"Really? So let me get this straight, Mr Brennan. You think that Sammi was, what, murdered?"

"That I do."

"And you have this expertise because you—?"

"He was a New York homicide detective, Alan. At least hear him out."

Alan looked from Sarah, then back to Jack. "This isn't New York. Or maybe you haven't noticed that?"

"Oh, I have. As a detective, you're kinda trained to notice a lot of things. Just telling you what I saw."

"Alan — do you know why Sammi came back?" Sarah said.

There you go, Jack thought. Great question, and maybe catching good old officer Alan off guard.

"No. I mean we couldn't rightly ask her, now could we?"

"And her mum, dad? Did you—?"

Sarah had leaned close, pressing with her questions. Jack was reminded that this was personal for Sarah; Sammi had been her friend.

"Course we did. They hadn't heard a word. Seems Sammi arrived and went to the Ploughman. Had a few before her accident. That was the last anyone saw her."

Jack cleared his voice. "So she just appeared back in the village, for no reason? Then had her accident?"

Alan looked right at Jack now. *Not a happy camper,* he thought. "Y'know, this is none of your affair. So you…" then to Sarah: "And *you,* best not go around stirring things up. This is police business."

Jack stood up.

The office felt tiny, claustrophobic. The scale of everything in the village seemed small, from the tables at Huffington's that were so close together that getting out to pay the bill was a strategic exercise, to the narrow alleyways between buildings off the main street.

"Right. Police business." Jack smiled, as Sarah got up as well. "We just thought you should know, that maybe you'd want to tell someone that Sammi didn't just drown."

"Speculation. Total speculation."

Jack gave him another nod, but didn't answer. He didn't know what to make of Alan the Policeman, who didn't seem at all curious about a local death. But clearly there was nothing to be gained from talking to him anymore.

"Thanks," Jack said, "for the time."

And he walked out with Sarah, thinking… *this is getting even more interesting. And suspicious.*

7.

TEA WITH MUM AND DAD

SARAH LOOKED AT JACK, sitting on the shabby couch in the cramped flat.

Jack gave her a smile that seemed to say… *can we move this along?*

Then she turned back to Sammi's mum who sat across from them, a tattered napkin clutched tight in the woman's one hand and a tea cup in the other that she sipped between bursts of tears.

They had decided that visiting the parents was the best place to start in order to find out what Sammi was doing back in Cherringham, despite Alan's assurances that her parents knew nothing.

"Y-you sure I can't fix you a cup. I can——"

"No, thank you, Mrs Charlton. We're fine."

"I'm good," Jack added.

From the slight slur in Mrs Charlton's words and the glassiness of the woman's eyes, Sarah was pretty sure that her cup contained more than tea.

Sammi always said she used to come back from school to find her mum half-sloshed, with her father racing to catch up as soon as he got home from work.

"Mr Charlton be here soon?" Sarah asked.

The woman nodded. "Yes, they got him doing extra hours at the poultry factory." A small smile from the woman. "He was never one to turn down a bit extra, you know. Even after th-this…"

And what is *this* to them? thought Sarah.

Did they see Sammi at all? Sammi had always said that she never wanted to see them again once she left for the bright lights of London. Yet she had been back to the village on her last night.

Sarah wasn't at all sure how to get information from this wreck of a woman. After a few moments of total awkwardness, Jack jumped in.

"Mrs Charlton," he said slowly, as if it might take the woman a few seconds to shift her orientation from Sarah to the tall American sitting in her minuscule sitting room. "I'm helping Sarah here look into a few things. I live on the river, on a boat, near where they found Sammi."

The woman again nodded.

Another quick smile, a disarming expression from Jack. Watching him, Sarah thought that he must have interrogated a lot of hard cases back in New York. This must be terribly odd for him, like being dropped into a BBC mystery series.

"Your Sammi came back here on Monday night, to the village and had her… accident."

The woman's head bobbed, waiting for the question.

"Did she come by and see you or your husband?"

The police had asked that question, Alan had told them. Sarah guessed that Jack must have a reason for asking it again.

Quickly the woman shook her head. The napkin did a few more serpentine runs through her fingers, soon to break off into ratty pieces. This was hard to watch.

"No. We didn't know she was coming at all, and she didn't come to see us."

On cue, the front door swung open.

And Mr Charlton stormed in, his face twisted into a dark scowl.

JACK TURNED TO the man who had entered the small sitting room as if it was a cage. Charlton's eyes darted from his wife, to Sarah, and finally to Jack.

"What's *this*? What the 'ell is going on here, anyways? You the damn police or what?"

"No. Mr Charlton. I'm just helping Sarah here."

The man looked away, rolling his eyes as if he couldn't believe his ears.

"A Yank." Then back to Jack. "A goddamn *Yank*. What are we doing, running a bed and breakfast here?"

"Malcolm, they just wanted to ask about Sammi, if we saw her and—"

Jack watched Charlton take a step towards him. He guessed from the slight wobble in that step that he had stopped off at a pub for a pint or three on the way home from the poultry factory.

Jack debated standing up but had a hunch he might get more — or at least *something* — from the man if he remained sitting instead of challenging him for what little open floor space there was.

"Sarah's concerned about her friend," Jack said. "And I was, well, just helping. You wife was saying that Sammi didn't come here."

"Good thing, too," the man said, a near bellow. "The amount of money that conniving bitch got from us? And a lot of it," — he fired a glare at his wife — "behind my back when old softie here posted her some. Put a stop to that, I did!"

"Borrowed a lot?"

"Stole too, things missing all the time." Another look towards the wife whose crying had been replaced with a totally cowed expression. "Like your mum's ring, right Ruth? Real diamond in it, and all. Gone."

The man sniffed the air. No mourning going on here, Jack thought.

"So you didn't know she had come back to the village the other night, and you didn't see her, is that right?"

Malcolm fixed Jack with a bullish glare. "You got ears, ain't ya? We didn't see her, I told you. And if she had—"

Jack raised his eyebrows.

"If she had—"

But Malcolm caught himself as though realizing that his alcohol-lubricated words were going to trip him up.

The man stopped. "Time for my tea. And time for you lot to leave us be. To—" the sarcasm was obvious — "mourn our lovely daughter's passing. In other words: get out."

And at that, Jack stood up, his height leaving mere inches between him and the ceiling.

"Well, thank you for your help… Mrs Charlton, Mr Charlton."
Sarcasm can work both ways.

Sarah stood up, looking a bit rattled with the exchange. But Jack saw that she had plastered a small smile on her face as she followed him outside. Where they both took deep breaths of the air, free from the stench of cigarettes, cheap whisky and bile.

Standing by Sarah's Rav4, Jack shot a look back at the beehive of flats.

"Nice folks," he said.

Sarah nodded. "Sammi gave them a hard time. Still, they were rough."

"And old Malcolm sounds as if he was — is — mighty upset with his daughter."

"You don't think—?"

"Think? We're just finding out things, Sarah, yes? Tell me, do you have time for another stop?"

"I can check on the kids. But they'll be okay for a bit longer, they'll be doing homework."

While Daniel and Chloe would have heard about the drowning, Sarah had decided not to tell them that she knew Sammi, that they had been best friends.

"What do you have in mind?" she said.

"Your friend officer Alan said that Sammi went to the pub. She must have had a reason. Let's go see if we can find out what that reason was. Okay?"

Sarah nodded. Then: "Thanks, Jack. She wasn't your friend. It's good of you, taking all this time."

He smiled at her. "No — what do you say — worries? Gets me out to see parts of the village that I might otherwise overlook. Besides — I like pubs."

She smiled back, and they both got into her car, heading to The Ploughman's, a pub that everyone seemed to visit at some point during the week.

8.

THE PLOUGHMAN

AT THE DOOR to the pub, the inside filled with Cherringham's thirstier inhabitants, Sarah reached out and touched Jack's elbow.

"Jack. This is a village pub, y'know."

He turned to her. "I have been here for a while."

"Yeah, the local. And they won't be too happy with anyone asking questions. Especially…"

"Oh. An *American*."

She nodded, and grinned. "Exactly. So maybe I'll ask the questions. And if I miss something…"

"I'll pass you a note."

And with that, Jack opened the door, and Sarah led the way in.

"Half a Boddington's please Billy," Sarah said.

She could see Jack hadn't understood a word she had said.

"Jack?"

Billy Leeper — who had been the main barman for as long as Sarah was legally able to come into the pub — was already pulling Sarah's beer.

"I'll have a pint," Jack said.

And when the barman put the two glasses down, she looked right at him. "Billy, guess you heard about Sammi?"

He nodded. "Bad business. Poor thing. You were mates back in the day, right?"

Sarah nodded. "Alan told us she was in here the night she died."

Sarah could sense that that question made Billy pull back a bit. "Yeah. Hard to recognize her, y'know? Looked like she'd gone through some rough times. Bit battered, know what I mean?"

"Yes, I—"

But then Billy was summoned by a trio of men at the end of the bar. Sarah caught them looking back at her, maybe wondering what she was doing with the fifty-year-old Jack.

Jack leaned a little close, his voice low. "Find out who, if anyone, she spoke to."

"I know, I know. I'll get to it. If he comes back…"

Billy was having a laugh with the guys in jeans and denim shirts, sleeves rolled up tight.

Then the barman gave a nod in Sarah's direction, and she felt even more conspicuous.

"This is so awkward," she said, her voice low.

"Hang in there. Sip the beer. He'll be back."

And after what seemed like a long time, Billy Leeper walked away from that end of the bar, back to Sarah.

Perhaps he thought it would look odd if he didn't come back when she had just started talking about Sammi's death.

"Yeah, poor girl. Sammi, God. Heard she got into some bad stuff up in London. But then," — a grin showed that Billy had lost a few teeth on his journey to be the Ancient Barman — "who wouldn't?"

"Billy, did she talk to anyone when she was here?"

The barman's eyes went from Sarah, to Jack, then back again. His face lost its puffy geniality. Now the eyes narrowed.

Even though this was Sarah's village, she too had been gone a long time. This isn't exactly *my* local anymore, Sarah thought.

At least not yet.

"Yeah. I mean, I passed a few words with her. She seemed distracted. But then Robbo came in, and it was like — well, like they'd been looking for each other."

Jack looked at Sarah. Probably wanted to know who Robbo was. *Time for that when we get out of here,* Sarah thought.

Robbo. Sammi's old boyfriend had a temper, and didn't mind showing it. Sarah had steered clear of him since she had come back to Cherringham.

On the rare night that Sarah did stop here, Robbo could be found just sitting in the corner, putting away the pints, glaring at her. He knew that Sarah had warned Sammi to stay away from him.

Over tea one afternoon, Grace told Sarah that he and his mates had got into some legal trouble, something about drugs.

Could be just gossip — but Sarah wouldn't have been surprised if it had turned out to be true.

"They just talk?" she said. "Here?"

"They went to a table in the back room. That time of night, no one eating dinner. But boy — you could hear them out here. I remember this quite clearly cuz it was the second half of the England-Germany game. No one was walking away from that match, I can tell you."

A voice called to Billy, and he moved away to another customer.

"Robbo?" Jack said. "Who's this Robbo?"

"Her ex. Nasty bit of work."

"Yeah. Not feeling any warmth for him from you." He gave her a smile. "You're doing great, by the way. Keep going."

40

Billy came back. "That's about all I can——"

"Did they stay here?"

"No. Like I said, everyone was watching the game, and the two of them, I saw them storm out of here, Sammi, then Robbo following. All steamed up. You know how he gets. I mean, he's been a little better since his run in with the police. Has to watch it. But that night — it was the old Robbo."

So there had been police trouble. She'd have to find out about that. Billy's words made her feel chilled.

If Robbo had been angry, anything could happen.

"They just walked out?"

Billy nodded. "Never came back. Could see them out in the car park. Talking, I guess. Maybe fighting. Then, when I looked again, they was gone."

He wiped the wood bar with a cloth as if signalling that the interview had ended.

"Another round for you two?"

Sarah looked at Jack to see whether he felt there was more to gain here though she felt that Billy had told what he knew.

Not that it was that much.

"Not for me," Jack said.

Billy had his eyes on Jack as if he maybe knew the American might be pulling the strings here.

"I'm good too——" She put down her beer, half finished.

And with the locals' eyes following them as if they were Russian spies and this was the Cold War, she and Jack left the pub, for the cool summer's night air outside.

She had the thought, tinged with a bit of alarm…

What exactly are we doing here?

And more… where will it lead?

Once outside, Jack said. "Quick dinner? Compare notes?"

Sarah checked her watch.

"Sorry Jack," Sarah said. "After last night, I told the kids I'd be home to cook their tea."

Jack smiled at that. "No problem. How about I call you later?"

"Sure. You think we should talk to Robbo?"

"Oh yes. Do you know where he works?" As she shook her head he said, "Well then any chance you can track it down? We'll give him a visit tomorrow."

"Can I give you a lift?" said Sarah.

"I'm fine. Nice evening for a walk. Now you get home."

With a nod, he turned and headed towards the toll bridge. Sarah watched him casually lope away down the hill.

Dinner? When was the last time anyone suggested she go out for dinner?

9.

DOWN ON THE FARM

SARAH SAT IN THE window seat in Huffington's and sipped her coffee. Thursdays she usually only went into the office after lunch — though in practice that didn't mean taking a morning off.

It just meant a half-day at home doing the week's washing, cleaning the kitchen floor, sorting the bedrooms, doing a supermarket run, then looking at the weeds in the front garden and realizing she'd once again run out of time to deal with them.

So today was a genuine morning off. Unless being a Private Detective counted as work, she thought.

In front of her she had a notepad filled with scribbles about Sammi, and what she'd learned in the last few days. *Notepads solve crimes,* Jack had said to her.

She doubted that, but it was amazing how much she'd learned about Sammi's life in the last twenty-four hours. And about other people in the village too.

A few phone calls to friends had unlocked some pretty unsavoury stories about Robbo. Complaints from girlfriends about violence — most of which never seemed to go to court.

No witnesses.

Or witnesses that never turned up.

The most recent had ended in a three-month sentence for punching a girl in a club. He'd only just come out of jail and was on probation, working on a farm a few miles out of the village.

It was unlikely he'd told the farm manager about the prison spell — that was Jack's theory when she'd brought him up to speed on the phone. So maybe that gave them some leverage if they were going to have a little chat.

A horn sounded. She looked up.

A little green sports car pulled up in the village square car park opposite. Austin Healey Sprite — top down, nice car, she thought. The driver waved — it was Jack, aviator shades on in the bright morning sunshine and looking much too big for the two-seater.

This was a surprise — Jack in a classic sixties sports car?

She drained her coffee, grabbed her notebook and went out.

As she crossed the road and climbed in the car, she didn't have to look behind her to know that the Huffington's regulars were already deep in conversation about her developing relationship with 'the American'.

And as they pulled away fast into the traffic, she resisted the urge to give a regal wave to the congregation. Or would that be two fingers…?

With the top down, the car was too noisy to chat. In the brief pause while they waited at the traffic lights at the top of the High Street, Jack asked for directions.

"Left here onto the main road, then there's a turn after a couple of miles. I'll give you a shout."

The lights changed, and with a gravely roar, they sped east away from Cherringham.

AT BARELY WALKING pace, Jack edged the Sprite towards the

tight bend, leaning forward in his seat to get a better view. The dry stone walls on each side of the narrow country lane were topped with hedges so it was impossible to see if anyone was coming the other way.

And it was his experience in England that when someone did come the other way, they were usually going at twice the speed limit.

"Want me to drive?" said Sarah next to him.

"No, I can handle it," he said, trying not to frown.

"Plenty of room for people to pass."

"Not how I see it from here."

"Never mind," she said. "We've got all day."

Jack flashed a quick glance at her. Was she teasing him? Maybe.

Kath used to tease him just like this. For being cautious.

That's how I survived thirty years on the streets, madam, without once getting shot, he used to tell her.

Sure it's not because you were always the last one to arrive? She used to counter.

But today he had a different passenger. And as long as they built roads better suited to horses than cars in this country, he was going to drive how he liked.

The road finally widened, giving glimpses of the countryside. Jack had never been up here. It was mostly pasture, dotted with the odd farm building made of heavy honey-coloured stone.

In the distance he could see far hills, and also the outlines of the massive hangars of RAF Belton, one of the busiest military airbases in the country.

This wasn't the Cotswolds that the tourists came to see. It wasn't chocolate box — it was agri-business. And in the winter, it would be bleak and windy up here.

"Turn left at the T," said Sarah.

He did as he was told.

"There's Clay Farm," she said, pointing to a wide gate and a gravel track, leading to a featureless 'sixties detached farmhouse. He swung the car off the lane and headed for a concrete apron in front of some hay barns where heavy tractors and trailers were parked.

The place seemed empty.

He turned the engine off. From behind one of the barns came the sound of heavy machinery.

"You do the talking again?" he said to Sarah.

"Sure," she said.

She looked nervous, he thought, as they climbed out of the car.

"This guy Robbo's no big deal, Sarah," he said.

"You don't need to tell me that. If it looks like I'm going to hit him, you stop me, okay?"

Jack nodded — and told himself to stop making assumptions about her. She could handle herself. Or at least — she believed she could.

She headed round the back of the nearest barn, and he followed.

SARAH RECOGNISED ROBBO straight away, even with his back to her. Tall and wiry, with long black hair — tied up and shoved into an orange hard-hat. "My Italian good looks" he used to call it at school. Not that he'd even been to Italy.

He was standing next to a bright green wood chipper, lazily feeding in chopped branches from a great pile on the concrete. The machine noisily ate the wood and spurted out chips into a hopper.

Sarah walked carefully around him so as not to startle him and motioned to him to turn off the machine.

Without taking his eyes off her, he leaned in and pressed a button and the machine clattered to a halt. He removed his hat and pulled out some earplugs, his eyes flicking across to take in Jack too.

"Well, if it ain't the Admiral's daughter," he said, leaning back against the machine.

"Robbo."

"What's this then? After a bit of farmyard action?"

Sarah hadn't spoken to him in twenty years but in an instant his school bullying came back to her. Not that he'd ever got one over on her or Sammi, she remembered.

"It's been a while, hasn't it?"

He shrugged and turned his attention to Jack.

"Bit old for her mate, aren't you? I hope you know where she's been."

Sarah watched Jack smile — how was he going to react to that?

"Robbo — you okay me calling you 'Robbo'?" said Jack.

Robbo looked confused for a second by Jack's politeness. He shrugged.

"Good," said Jack. He took a small step closer. "So here's the thing, *Robbo*. Remember you were down at the Ploughman's the other night?"

"I might have been."

"Anyway — Robbo — it turns out you were the last person to see our friend Sammi alive."

"What's this about? Who the hell are you anyway?"

"You see — not long after you and Sammi left the pub, she turned up dead in the river. Course you know that. He knows that, Sarah, doesn't he?"

Sarah saw the way Jack was going to play this.

"Oh, I think he does, Jack. Robbo's a clever guy. He watches a lot of TV. You watch TV, don't you, Robbo? Crime shows?"

"Maybe. But I don't see what —"

"So Robbo, you know that it's always the last person to see the victim who gets the blame," said Sarah.

She smiled, so reasonable.

"Blame? Blame for what?" said Robbo. He was looking confused now, like a boxer who's been hit and can't quite remember the routine.

"Blame for murder, of course," said Jack.

Robbo blinked hard.

"Who says she was murdered? She fell in, didn't she? Everybody knows that."

"That's not what the cops are saying now, Robbo," said Jack. "They're thinking maybe it was murder all along. And what with you being on probation—"

"How do you know about that?" He looked around anxiously. "You can't go round saying crap like that — and who are you anyway?"

Robbo started to move from side to side, agitated. Sarah took a step back.

This is like a game of Pop Goes the Weasel, she thought.

"Robbo — you mean you haven't told your boss about being on probation?" she said. "You really ought to — I mean really."

She saw his hands tighten into fists.

"Don't be stupid, you stupid—" He caught himself. "If he heard about that I'd lose my job."

There. Robbo's confidence had evaporated. Sarah felt totally in control. She looked across at Jack who nodded discreetly. Time to turn the screw...

"You've got more to worry about than your job, Robbo. We're talking murder — remember?"

"I didn't kill her. I just talked to her!"

"When was that, then, Robbo? At the pub?"

Robbo's eyes darted from her to Jack and back again.

"If I tell you this stuff — can you get the police off my back?"

"Sure, Robbo," said Sarah. "All we want to do is find out who killed Sammi. We don't want the police to go round wasting time investigating innocent people."

Robbo breathed deeply.

"All right. This is what happened. I was watching the game on the big screen down at the Ploughman's. With the lads, you know? Anyway she comes in, all kissy-kissy. I hadn't seen her in a couple of years. She wanted to score, didn't she? Like she was all nervous about something."

Robbo sniffed as if his own nostrils also got a regular workout.

"And?" Sarah said.

"So anyway I had some — and I said she could do a line. I didn't sell it mind, I'm not a dealer. Then she starts arguing, laying into me, giving me all kinds of crap. So I grabs hold of her, takes her outside."

"So you went out to the car park?" said Jack.

"Yeah. She calms down after a bit and we go for a bit of a walk. Went and sat in her car."

"She had a car?" said Sarah.

"Yeah. New one from the smell of it."

"What make was it Robbo?" said Jack.

"I dunno, I was doing a line wasn't I, not buying the bleedin' car!"

"So what happened then?" said Sarah quickly.

"We got in the car, all smiles again. Did a line each. Had a laugh. She said she'd come back to the village to sort some bloke out. Some rich bloke who was treating her like trash, she said."

"Did she say who?" said Sarah.

"I didn't ask her, now did I? None of my damn business. I thought maybe me and her might get it off, know what I mean?"

"But you didn't?" said Jack.

"Nah."

"And this guy — did she say anything about him?" said Sarah.

"Nah. Just that he was loaded. Had some swanky place in London."

"But he was local?"

"Think so."

"So what happened then?" said Jack.

"She went all teary — and I hate that. So I told her I was going back to the pub."

"What time was that?" said Sarah.

"Dunno. 'Bout midnight. Bleedin' pub was shut when I got back so I went home. And we lost the match. Crap evening altogether."

"Yeah, wasn't so great for Sammi, either," said Sarah.

"So when you last saw her, Robbo — where was she?" said Jack.

"Sitting in her car crying," said Robbo. "Useless, she was."

Sarah looked at his whimpering face and felt the anger surge in her stomach. All she wanted to do now was to push him up against his chipping machine and punch him as hard as she could — for Sammi.

She felt Jack's hand on her shoulder.

"I reckon Robbo's told us what we need, Sarah, don't you? If he's forgotten anything, we can always come back and have a wee chat with him. Or his boss."

She watched as Jack turned to Robbo, put a gentle hand on his shoulder and fixed him hard and long.

"You won't mind that, Robbo, will you? It could be very awkward if you've not been honest with us."

And as she watched Robbo, she saw that he was cowed by what he'd seen in Jack's eyes.

"No, I won't mind. I've told you the truth, I have."

Sarah watched as Jack smiled at him before turning to her.

"Come on, Sarah. Don't know about you but I could use some

fresh air."

And together they headed back to the car.

MURDER ON THAMES

10.

GOING NOWHERE

SARAH STARED MISERABLY at her computer screen. No matter how you cropped, tinted or framed them — pictures of coffins and hearses said only one thing...

Death.

Bassett and Son Funeral Directors. Why this job, this week of all weeks? When all she could think of was Sammi.

Floating in the river.

Lying on a mortuary slab.

Too grim, she thought.

And she had got nowhere with Robbo's information. Laura in the estate agents' downstairs had pointed her at various land registries and sales sites for the local area — but trying to find the right rich Cherringham sugar daddy with a place in London was impossible.

There were nearly three thousand people in the village and she just didn't have enough to go on.

She looked at the clock. Six o'clock. Grace had gone home. And at seven she and the children were supposed to be going over to mum and dad's for supper.

Everyone on best behaviour, interrogations about school results, and all those questions…

Was she seeing anyone, how did she cope in that little house? Surely she'd be happier moving back in with them! Had she been in touch with Oliver? No marriage is ever too broken that it can't be put back together…?

She would have to brace herself.

The phone rang. She picked it up instantly.

"Yes?"

"Whoa. Whatever happened to hi?"

"Jack. Sorry. One of those days."

"Uh-huh? You tracked down our sugar daddy?"

"Needle in a haystack. You know how many wealthy people live in this area, and so many of them with London flats as well. I need more to go on."

"I don't think we got more," said Jack. "Though I *was* thinking maybe we should have a chat with the lady who found Sammi. What was her name?"

"Lou Tidewell. She works at the charity shop. We could talk to her in the morning."

"Sure. We ought to catch up anyway."

On a whim, Sarah had an idea for making the evening bearable.

"Jack — what are you up to this evening? Fancy dinner? I'm going to my parents'. Mum's an interesting cook. And dad likes Americans."

There was a pause on the other end of the line.

"Why not? I haven't had home cooking in years."

"Great," she said. "I'll pick you up at seven"

She put the phone down and laughed to herself. Poor Jack. What had she just done?

MURDER ON THAMES

11.

FAMILY MATTERS

JACK CHEWED SLOWLY in the silence. At either end of the table, Sarah's mother Helen and her father Michael scrutinized him carefully. Across the table sat Sarah's two children, Chloe and Daniel, both wide-eyed and suppressing giggles.

And next to him, Sarah looked nervous.

They were sitting on the patio at the back of Sarah's parents' house in the late evening sunshine. The broad terrace gave onto a perfect lawn which swept in a gentle slope down toward the Thames itself.

Real nice spot, he thought.

Jack had decided on collar, tie and sports jacket — and he knew it had been the right decision.

"I'm guessing... I think I'm tasting... dates?" said Jack.

"Oh, *very* good," said Helen.

"And tuna? No, no, wait a minute — anchovy? In balsamic vinegar?"

"Bravo Jack!" said Michael. "That's a first, Helen — nobody's ever unravelled your salad dressing before!"

"Quite an unusual combination, don't you think Jack?" said Sarah. "I bet you never had that in New York?"

Jack smiled at her. She knew exactly what he was going through.

"No," he said. "I don't think I've ever encountered one quite like this."

And that was certainly true. Sarah's mother had created possibly the worst — and yet strangely the most imaginative — food he'd ever had the misfortune to eat.

"One of the rewards of being a services family, Jack," said Michael. "Every three years uprooted and flown somewhere new. Airbases. Embassies. Far East, Middle East, all points east."

"So *many* influences on my cooking!" said Helen proudly.

"Must have been so difficult for you, Sarah" said Jack, returning the irony. He took a good swig of wine. He was daring her to laugh and she was having a hard time fighting it.

"Nonsense," said Michael. "All that travelling — Sarah's picked up life skills that are the envy of her peers!"

"That true?" said Jack.

"Yeah, it is," said Daniel. "My mum knows how to fire a machine gun and drive a truck!"

"Very good Daniel," said Michael. "Though I think the technical term is 'strip an SA80'."

Sarah shrugged.

"In Cyprus, some of the men in the regiment thought it might come in handy one day."

"Can't quite see you in uniform, Sarah," said Jack.

"Not for want of my trying, eh?" said Michael. "In the end she got too much of a handful and we shipped her home. Then I retired from the RAF and we came back here. And we've never regretted it, have we darling?"

"Never!" said Helen. "Our little corner of paradise — I'm sure you agree?"

"It's very pleasant," said Jack.

And it truly was. Sarah had warned him her parents liked everything "just so" and the big, white-stuccoed house and gardens were the evidence. Though the RAF had given her father a good pension, he'd still been young enough when he retired to start a consultancy business advising Middle Eastern governments on defence contractors apparently which clearly now made extremely good money. Jack knew better than to ask too many questions, though Helen and Michael had no such qualms about interrogating him. In fact he had to admit they'd got pretty much everything out of him — his New York background, the police, the boat, Riley, how he met Sarah, even his immigration status...

Made him wonder who the ex-cop around here was. But he knew they hadn't finished.

"So Jack, I do hope you don't think I'm being rude, but is there no Mrs Brennan in your life?" said Helen.

Jack had been waiting for this question, though when it came it was never easy.

"There was, Mrs Edwards. She died two years back. Cancer."

"Oh, I'm sorry," said Helen.

Jack became aware that the table had now gone quiet. That "C" word — whisper it, avoid it, say it loud — it always had the same chilling effect.

"It's okay. In fact, that's kinda how I ended up down on the river. Kath and I came here together thirty years ago. Loved the place. Always planned to retire here. So when she died, that's what I did. Only without her."

"Well, I'm sure it's... all for the best," said Helen awkwardly.

No matter how many times Jack told this simple story, it always led to silence.

There's got to be a better way to say it, but I'm damned if I know how, he thought.

56

"Come on kids — let's clear this away," said Sarah, rising to her feet and beginning to pile plates.

Jack could see that the kids couldn't wait.

SARAH WATCHED HER father and Jack chatting easily. After supper was over, they'd all moved down the garden to the little deck by the river where her parents set up comfy chairs under a gazebo in summer.

The kids were now inside watching TV. On the far side of the river, the sun was going down over Cherringham. And on the opposite bank, the smart river cruisers were alight with conversation and the chink of glasses.

The conversation had shifted to Sammi.

"All I'm saying is, tread carefully," said her father. "This village needs tourists — and nobody likes talk of a murder. Especially when it's a couple of outsiders stirring things."

"I'm hardly an outsider, Dad," said Sarah.

Her father topped up his glass with red wine.

"You may have gone to school here — but you left. Which makes you an outsider again."

"How long was I away? Fifteen years? That's nothing."

"Regardless. That's how they'll see you if they want. Same with you Jack — an American trampling around. They won't like that at all. No offence."

"Well, they'll just have to put up with it," said Sarah. "Sammi was my friend and if somebody killed her, they need to be caught."

"She was an accident waiting to happen, Sarah, that's what we always said, didn't we darling?" said Michael, looking to Sarah's mother for support.

Sarah started to fume inside.

This was why she could never, ever come back to live with her parents, they could be *so* judgemental — and Sammi had been her *best* friend, did her mother not remember that?

"You're right, of course Michael," said Jack. "Nothing worse than small-town politics eh?"

"Spot on," said Michael.

Sarah looked daggers at Jack. Could he not see she needed some support here?

"So tell me," Jack continued. "The big boats over there — they ever bother you?"

Her father turned to look at the boats.

"No, they keep themselves to themselves to be honest. We get the odd noisy dinner party, but the kind of people who moor up down here are usually looking for a bit of peace and quiet."

"Locals, are they?"

"Not necessarily. Some of them come down here for a weekend or a week at the most. A lot cruise all the way from London, then head back downriver on a Sunday night."

"Need quite a few bob for a mooring, I expect?" said Jack.

"It's expensive enough here, as I'm sure you know. But up in London they'll be paying ten or twenty grand a year."

Jack caught Sarah's eye — and she suddenly realized what he was suggesting.

Sammi's sugar daddy didn't necessarily have to own a flat up in London.

He might own a boat.

And that would make him a lot easier to track down. Just a question of matching boat registers to the electoral register in Cherringham.

She nodded back to him and realized she'd completely forgotten her fury at her father. It had been a good idea to ask Jack along.

Because we just got a breakthrough.

WHILE SARAH PILED the kids into the Rav4, Jack said his thanks and goodbyes to Mr and Mrs Edwards who now stood in the doorway of the house.

"Will we be seeing you on Saturday, Jack?" said Helen. "At the concert?"

"Oh. I hadn't planned—".

"Dear me, do you mean Sarah hasn't asked you?" she continued. "We're doing Leoncavallo's *Pagliacci*. Not the whole thing, of course! Excerpts. The best morsels!"

"It's a fine piece," said Jack.

"An opera buff too, Jack? Full of surprises," said Michael.

"For an American — or a cop?" said Jack.

"Both!" said Michael.

Jack laughed — Sarah's father said what he felt, a trait he'd already noted in his daughter. No wonder they kept butting up against each other.

"It's in the village hall at seven o'clock sharp, I'll put a ticket aside for you," said Helen. "If we even go on, of course — our lead soprano's sick and missed our last rehearsal on Monday night, so fingers crossed or — Lord save us — yours truly will be taking the part!"

"I'm sure Jack's looking forward to it already, Mum," said Sarah, kissing her mother goodnight.

Jack bid his farewells and promised Sarah he'd call first thing. He wanted to walk back to his boat along the river.

Interesting dinner. There was a lot to think about. And just as he had on the streets of Manhattan, he liked to do his thinking alone.

12.

COVER GIRL

SARAH GOT INTO the office early.

She saw a large envelope on her desk. She opened it and pulled out some glossy layouts and a note from Grace.

'I know you're having a hard time with Bassett and Son so I thought I'd have a go at it. What do you think? Any good?'

They were better than good, Sarah thought. Perfect — not a coffin in sight. All ethereal mist and river scenes — almost made death an attractive lifestyle choice.

Well, maybe not... *life*style.

Good start to the day — made even better with an email from her friend Gary in London. During the worst of the break-up with Oliver, she'd used Gary's data skills to nail her ex-husband's fraudulent behaviour.

Anything digital — and Gary could find it. And find it he had...

She'd called him when she got back from her parents' the night before with the theory about the boat registry. Gary had matched the registers and come out with half a dozen names of Cherringham citizens with London-registered boats.

Only three were in the country. One of those was in his nineties.

Another was probably out of the question because he had a male partner. But the third was very interesting.

Gordon Williams. Millionaire owner of Imperial SuperYachts. Registered owner of a fifty-foot luxury cruiser moored at St Katherine's Dock, Tower Bridge. He was currently residing at Imperial House, Lower Runstead. Just five miles along the river from Cherringham.

Was this Sammi's sugar daddy?

Sarah left a "thank you" note for Grace, rang Jack with the news and headed out of the office at speed.

IN SPITE OF SARAH'S complaints, Jack insisted on driving.

"Come on — I need the practice," he said, grinning.

She had called Williams expecting him to have no interest in meeting. *Isn't that what someone — a sugar-daddy with something to hide -- would do?* But Williams said they could come over immediately.

It was still early so they had to queue to get over the Cherringham Toll Bridge — which Jack still thought was one of the weirdest things he'd encountered since coming to live here.

The bridge was medieval. And since medieval times, one family (the Bucklands) had somehow collared the right to charge every cart, pony, car and truck that wanted to cross the river and head up the road to Cherringham.

Two old ladies sat in a small windowed hut at the end of the bridge, duly taking twenty pence from every driver.

From dawn to dusk.

Amazing.

There was always a queue. And every time he sat in the queue, Jack did the sums. And every time he concluded that the Buckland family must be clearing nearly a million a year on the toll bridge.

Who were the two old ladies? Were they Bucklands? And if so —

what the hell did they do with all that money?

At least the way to Runstead was via a proper road, with white lines and speed limits. And on the way, Sarah filled him in on her phone call.

Williams knew Sammi. He was saddened to hear about Sammi's death. And he only had a one-hour window so could they please be prompt…

LOWER RUNSTEAD TURNED out to be one of those sleepy little villages where you never see a soul on the street.

Jack drove carefully past trim-stone cottages and high hedges, until Imperial House came into view, set back behind tall sweeping walls and a pair of imposing spiked iron gates.

When they drew up, the gates opened automatically. Mr Williams clearly had security who were on the ball.

As they drove up the long gravel drive, Jack guessed that once upon a time, Imperial House had been the old manor house, given a modern make-over. Extensions front, back and sides — and probably a pool and gym in the basement.

"Not for the likes of you and me, Jack," said Sarah beside him.

"And let us thank God for that," said Jack. "Just look at all that shrubbery."

They rounded a fountain, nestled on perfect lawn, and pulled up next to a big black mud-spattered Range Rover Sport. Jack took note. A young guy in T-shirt and jeans, tall and nonchalant, stood beside the vehicle, hosing it down.

Jack noticed how the guy smiled at Sarah as she got out of the car. And how Sarah smiled back.

"Nice car," said Jack. "Must go like a rocket, huh?"

"And some," the young guy said. "When I get to drive it, that is."

"We're looking for Mr Williams," said Sarah, joining him.

"Just ring the bell. Someone'll come."

But before they could, the front door opened and a tall, bronzed figure emerged. Pink polo shirt, classy chinos, snakeskin belt, Rolex watch: Jack knew this was the boss — Gordon Williams.

And he also knew instantly the relationship with Mr Car Wash.

"Dad — you want me to do the inside too?" said the boy. The son's tone showed no enthusiasm for the task.

"No, that'll do, Kaz," said Williams, pausing for a second. "Pop it in the garage would you when you're done? Good lad."

His son nodded and carried on cleaning.

Williams approached, hand outstretched to greet them.

"Good of you both to come," he said, with a charming smile. "This way, we've got coffee on the terrace."

Hardly stopping, he led them all the way round the side of the house to where a series of terraces led down to the river and a perfect view of meadows and woods beyond.

Jack took in the view. *'Good of you both to come,'* he'd said. As if *he'd* invited *them*. This guy was interesting…

A table and chairs with a big ivory parasol to shade it from the morning sun had been set up. A young woman in a maid's outfit stood ready to pour coffees and teas. Williams motioned them to sit and they all waited politely while the maid poured the drinks.

Jack watched as Williams with a practised micro-gesture of one finger instructed the servant to go.

"So, Miss Edwards. As I said on the phone, I'm happy to help — but I'm not sure there's much I can add about poor Sammi."

"I gather she worked for you, Mr Williams?" said Jack.

"Well, that's not really how it was," said Williams. "Sammi was the face of Imperial."

He picked up a brochure from the table and handed it to Sarah.

"We construct high-end luxury cruising yachts. And Sammi was our key model last year for the new "C" Class range. So she worked freelance with us really — not *for* us."

"So you didn't know her?" said Jack.

Williams hesitated. Then: "No, on the contrary, we got to know Sammi very well. We all spent a month together in the Maldives on the photo shoot."

"We?" said Sarah.

"My wife, Maureen. My son Kaz — who you just met."

"Isn't that unusual? She was just the model, wasn't she?" said Jack.

Williams smiled at Sarah.

"You knew her didn't you, Miss Edwards? So you can understand how she soon became more than just a model on the shoot. Such a lovely girl, so generous and lively. She became a real friend. To all of us."

Jack tried to work out this little foursome, all at sea on a luxury boat. Interesting...

And unbelievable.

"You can imagine how terribly upset we were to hear of her death," Williams concluded.

"I'm sure," said Jack.

He waited — and hoped that Sarah wouldn't fill the silence.

She didn't. She was getting good at this.

A minute passed.

"So what exactly did you want to ask me?" said Williams. "I have a rather tight schedule you know, and I do need to get back to work."

"Ah, I see," said Jack. "I'm sorry — I thought my colleague here had already told you why we needed to see you?"

Williams shrugged.

"Well, no, not really, she just said it was about Sammi and she was an old friend."

Jack smiled and watched Williams carefully.

"Ah that explains it. Well, to get to the point, Mr Williams. You see, we believe Sammi was murdered. Possibly by a man in the local area with whom she was having an affair. And we wondered if you might know anything about that?"

Jack looked for the tell. Williams leaned forward, shocked.

"Murdered? But that's — if you believe this, you must go to the police straight away, Mr Brennan."

"We have," said Sarah.

"We were wondering where you were on the night that she died?" said Jack.

Williams grabbed the arms of his chair, his body instantly rigid.

"I'm not sure you have any right to ask me that."

"Guess we could suggest to the police that they ask you," Jack said.

Williams looked away, then back to Jack. "I was in London at the Boat Fair. And I assume from your question that you believe I am that 'man in the local area'?"

"We're not discounting anything, Mr Williams," said Sarah.

Williams got to his feet.

"Interview over, I'm afraid. You've obviously been very affected by Sammi's death. As we have too. But please — don't let your imagination run away with you. I was very fond of Sammi, and I certainly would never have wanted any harm to come to her."

As he spoke, Jack saw a woman emerging from the house.

Taller than Williams, elegant in skinny jeans and a white blouse, she was lean and tanned and in her fifties.

She came over and Williams went to her, put his arm around her.

"My wife, Maureen."

Jack nodded to her.

"Maureen — I'm afraid our guests are leaving. They have another engagement."

Mrs Williams looked surprised and disappointed.

"Oh. I'm sorry to have missed you. You were friends of Sammi's — isn't that right?"

"I was, Mrs Williams," said Sarah.

"So sad," said Mrs Williams. "She was such a pretty thing. A ray of light, isn't that right Gordy?"

Williams nodded, not taking his eyes off Jack.

"It's always the best that are taken away from us," continued Mrs Williams. "Don't you agree?"

Jack nodded.

"My condolences anyway to you," Mrs Williams continued. "So awful, what happened. We've been so very upset."

Williams gently ushered them away towards the side of the house.

Just before they rounded the building, Jack looked back and saw Mrs Williams wave sadly, then turn and look away to the far hills.

Did she really think Sammi was one of the 'best'?

Was 'Gordy' telling the truth?

The truth about Sammi — her life, her lover and her death — was proving to be as elusive as ever.

13.

THE PRINCIPLES OF MURDER

SARAH COULDN'T HELP but grab the edge of her seat as Jack drove.

Though it was a small car Jack still seemed to hug the hedges and approach every curve as if a tank was roaring at him from the other direction.

She caught him look at her.

"Nervous? Don't worry, Sarah — I'm getting the hang of this. Though those tunnels where you I — I dunno—"

"Give way?"

"Right. Those seem like they were designed for accidents."

"We get our share."

"People should honk, or something—"

"Not very British, that. People are just expected to know how to…"

"'Give way'. Right, ESP."

She waited a few moments as he negotiated another corner.

"Jack, you have any ideas about what just happened? With Williams?"

"I'm thinking."

"How about we stop for a pint and you can think aloud? There's a sweet riverside pub just ahead, The Swan."

"You got it. Though you may not like what I'm thinking."

And Sarah forced her hands to release the death-grip on her bucket seat as they hit the straight, probably Roman road that led to the pub just ahead.

AS IF IT was a prop, a lone swan, looking sooty and dishevelled, circled near them as they sat at a picnic table right on the edge of the water.

"Guess she's looking for a hand-out. Food here any good? Never been."

"Think they can manage the staples. Fish, chips. Sunday roast."

She watched him take a sip of his beer, still quiet, as if expecting her to push him with questions. Maybe all detectives — real ones at least — kept their thoughts to themselves.

But they were in this together.

So push she did.

"You found nothing suspicious about Gordon Williams?"

"Did I say that? Suspicions? Everybody has those. And no, I'm not buying the 'happy family travelling with the young cover girl'. I can easily imagine that old Gordy had other less wholesome interests in your friend."

"Then — he might have a motive for killing Sammi!"

"You see a conclusion and you do like to jump, hmm?"

He grinned at her, and she realized what an amateur she must sound like.

"It's something, isn't it?"

"Well, we've had nothing until now. Although Robbo looked as guilty as hell despite there being no evidence. Or motive."

"That we know of."

"Touché. Then there's Sammi's dear old dad with his money issues. As to Gordy, could it be an affair gone wrong? Possibly. But despite wanting us out of there *asap* when our questions turned uncomfortable, I didn't see anything else. And if he said he was in London, then I imagine you can check that out pretty easily? Your computer friend, huh?"

"Probably."

She took a sip of her beer, the sun low in the sky, shining on them with a golden light.

Then: "What about Kaz?"

"Yes. The son washing the car. You mean, maybe he was involved somehow with Sammi?"

She immediately felt how little they had.

Another smile from Jack as if he had let her questions prove his point.

They had nothing.

"You still haven't told me what you think."

He looked away, squinting at the sun.

"Pretty pub this. This whole country's filled with them."

Then back.

"What do I think? I think it is just possible that Sammi did exactly what the police believe. She killed herself."

"No."

Jack's eyebrows went up.

"You yourself said she couldn't have drowned upriver."

"True. *That* didn't happen. But she had drugs in her. Wouldn't take much — a few gulps of water at the weir."

"And why at the weir?"

"Why not?"

She leaned across the table. "I know Sammi. And despite everything she'd gone through, whatever bad times she'd had in London, she wouldn't have killed herself."

"People can be pushed to the edge, Sarah."

Jack said those words as if he suspected that Sarah herself had faced some edges. Marriage, divorce, single parenthood.

None of that too pretty or too easy.

"Trust me. I knew her, she was my best friend."

Jack nodded. "Okay. I will do just that. So then that leaves…" he tilted his beer glass to her, "… murder."

"Right."

"And when you have nothing — which pretty much is what we have — then there is only one thing to do."

"I'm listening."

"Back to first principles of murder and investigation."

"This is feeling like master class."

"You can take notes if you like. But one of the first principles of any detective work is that if you hit a wall, if you have *nada*, and you're not seeing any next step, then it's back to what we pros call… 'square one'."

She laughed at this. He might get quiet sometimes but he could be funny once she got him talking.

"And what is 'square one' in this case?"

"You tell me, Sarah."

This IS a class.

She thought for a moment.

"The woman who found Sammi. Lou Tidewell."

"Exactly. We're assuming that she told the police all she saw. But that is an assumption, and assumptions can be fatal. Literally."

Jack downed his beer.

"So we need to talk to her."

But Jack shook his head. "No. *You* need talk to her."

"What — you have something better to do?"

"I do want to finish that fly. I mean, it is my intent to determine whether there really are any fish in this river. But —"

He put his empty glass down.

"Another?" she said.

He shook his head.

"I haven't met the woman, but I imagine if the two of us show up and one of us is an American with a lot of questions, it's possible we'll learn nothing. We have a far better shot if you go on your own. Ask questions. See if the police missed anything — or maybe she's remembered something since that could be important."

Sarah nodded. Though not at all sure she wanted to do this questioning herself, she also felt pleased that Jack thought she could do it.

"Kids all right for a bit?"

"I'll need to fix them tea in a bit. But I have time to stop at Lou's place. Not far from the weir. If she's home, I can try talking to her."

He nodded.

"And you — off to finish that fly?"

He shook his head. "Um, no. Actually I'm going to do something else."

"Which is?"

"In the interest of plausible deniability, best I tell you after I do it. In case something should happen."

"You're going to do something illegal?"

He looked at his watch, the sun now sitting at the horizon and a gentle breeze off the river that actually felt cool.

"Did I say that?"

He stood up. "We'll compare notes in the morning. Now I'll take you safely back to the village."

She followed him, leaving her pint half full. "And remember to 'give way'."

"Absolutely."

14.

SQUARE ONE

SARAH KNOCKED ON the cottage door. A small planter to the side of the entrance dripped with an assortment of colourful flowers. She heard the TV blaring from inside, and knocked a bit louder.

The TV went silent, and in second Lou Tidewell stood at the door.

While Sarah didn't know her well, the woman was a familiar sight in the village, with her dog and her rustic country dress. Any excuse to wear bright green Wellingtons.

Would she know Sarah at all? People in a village could be very careful about whom they talked to.

"Mrs Tidewell—" Sarah said as Lou opened the door.

"Sarah Edwards?"

That answered that question.

"Yes, Mrs Tidewell—"

"'Lou', please. Is there something wrong?"

Sarah looked at the woman at the door wondering if she could possibly have anything more to tell about the morning she found Sammi.

"I was wondering. It was my friend Sammi who you discovered. I was wondering if we could…" Sarah forced a smile, "… chat a bit."

The woman didn't smile back. "She was a friend of yours? Didn't know that. And I told the police everything."

But she stopped as if something about Sarah touched her. "Oh, all right then, come in."

Lou opened the door and led the way to the sitting room. A Chocolate Labrador raised its head sleepily as Sarah entered, and then lowered it as Lou indicated a chair with white lace antimacassars perfectly in place, as if waiting for the infrequent guest.

"Tea?" Lou said.

"That would be great."

Whatever was to come would certainly go easier with a cup of tea as a prop.

"SUCH A *TERRIBLE* thing. A young girl like that. And she was your best friend. So sad."

"Years ago," Sarah added. "We had fallen out of touch. Now I'm just trying to understand."

The woman nodded as if it that made sense.

Sarah wasn't sure it did.

"Don't know," Lou said, "what could possess someone to take their own life. I mean, we all have hard times, right? Somehow we carry on."

Did Lou in her role of village elder and general know-it-all have knowledge of Sarah's own tale?

She wouldn't be surprised.

Sarah put down her teacup and leaned close to Lou as if she was sharing a secret.

"But you see, that's just it. I don't think Sammi did take her own life. In fact, I'm sure of it."

The woman's eyes went wide.

"But the police seem quite certain that she drowned, that she must have jumped in and—"

Sarah nodded. "I know. I've spoken to them. Which is one reason I'm here. Is there anything you remember about what you saw that morning? Anything that you thought... odd?"

"I told the police everything, dear. I mean as soon as I saw it was a young girl, that she was dead..."

Lou's voice shook a bit, the memory clearly unpleasant. "I wanted to get as far away as possible. Forget the whole thing. So I don't think..."

Only minutes into the tea and conversation and it was beginning to seem that this interview was over.

So much for my solo detective work, thought Sarah.

"In fact, I haven't taken Brady there for his walk since. Don't know if I ever will."

Sarah nodded. How could she press on? Louella Tidewell had been through enough.

She was about to get up. Maybe things would have turned out differently if Jack had been here.

And then —

A detail.

"And she was dressed so beautifully."

Sarah stopped.

"She was? In what way?"

The woman's eyes met Sarah's, clearly picturing the scene.

"When I saw her, when I walked over, I could see how muddy it was there. It had been raining the day before. Such a mess! Muddy, the ground was, almost impossible to walk on."

"And Sammi?"

"Short for Samantha, I suppose. Such a pretty name. An old-fashioned name. Anyway. Such a *mess* all around her and there she

74

was in a beautiful top, sparkly. It caught the light even on that overcast morning. And her skirt. Smart, like you'd wear on, well, a date. Or to meet someone. She had only one shoe on. Such a sad thing to see. And not a shoe to go tromping around a muddy river."

"She was dressed to meet someone?"

"Why, that's certainly what it looked like."

A meeting. A rendezvous.

Could this be important Sarah thought? Another bit of evidence that said that Sammi didn't get all dressed up to jump in the river.

She was convinced that whomever Sammi got all dressed up for had to be the killer.

Then she caught herself. What was it Jack said about jumping and conclusions?

Still — it seemed important.

She gave the woman another smile. "Is there anything else?"

"No. I mean, I told you everything I saw. Now it's something to forget. Close my eyes — and I can still see her."

Sarah reached out and patted the woman's hand.

"Thank you for talking to me, Lou."

"Not much help I'm afraid. I mean, for you to understand."

Sarah stood up.

She looked down at the Labrador. "Beautiful dog."

"Brady? He's my old friend. My companion. Makes life worth living to have him by my side."

"Thanks again. I better get home — children to feed and all that."

"Yes. And you stay safe, dear."

Sarah nodded, and with a last smile, left the small cottage.

SARAH ENTERED THROUGH the kitchen door, twisting the knob

with one hand and holding a bag of quickly purchased groceries to fix the children's tea, only to see Chloe standing at the open fridge.

Her daughter spun around.

"Oh, Chloe, sorry, I'm running a bit late. But I got—"

Her daughter shut the fridge door with what seemed more force than necessary.

"Mum." Her voice was flat, disapproving. The chat with Lou Tidewell had gone on for a bit longer than Sarah had wanted.

Still, Sarah had texted to say that she was on her way and food was forthcoming.

"Where were you?"

"What do you mean?"

"I called your office. Grace said you hadn't been there for hours. Had some errands."

Divorce does unfair things to kids, Sarah knew. The kids would for ever be between Oliver and her, never knowing who to blame, who to trust…

Maybe who to love.

"I had work errands, Chloe. Some clients to meet—"

Her daughter took a few steps closer as Sarah put down the bag of shopping. "One of my friends said that you've been with that old American."

Sarah smiled at that. "He's not *that* old, and—"

"Mum!" Chloe said cutting her off. "What's going on?"

Teenage girls.

Always heard they could be a challenge, and I'm only just getting started with Chloe.

"Where's your brother?"

"Daniel's in his room, he's got some big project to do."

Sarah nodded. "So, you heard about the woman they found?"

"Yeah. The kids at school said she used to live round here. She drowned."

Sarah thought it best not to say too much. "I knew her."

Chloe's eyes went wide.

"We used to be, well, best friends. Years ago."

To make this easier, Sarah began to unpack the shopping bag, the wedge of cheddar, milk, macaroni, an onion. All the essentials for a quick macaroni cheese.

"And there were things I didn't understand. The American — that 'old' guy — is from New York. A retired detective. He's just helping me."

"You mean she didn't drown?"

Bag unpacked, now Sarah took a step closer and put a hand on her daughter's shoulder.

Won't be long before she's my height.

"No. I mean I'm not sure. But since she was my friend, I'd just like to know more. Why she came back here, what happened. That make sense?"

And finally Chloe nodded.

"Good. So now *that* mystery's solved, how about you help me whip up my famous macaroni cheese. I'm famished."

Chloe smiled.

Teenagers can be difficult but — apparently — they can also empathize.

"Sure."

The two of them set to fixing the quick dinner, and Sarah had only a passing thought about Jack, and when she could tell him of her chat with Lou Tidewell.

And learn exactly what he was doing that he didn't want her to know about.

15.

A CASE OF CARS

JACK HAD WAITED on his boat until the sky turned from a rich deep purple to a moonless black.

What he was about to do was better done at night.

It was a hunch. Despite his suggestion to Sarah that she avoid assumptions and conclusions, he himself had no problem about having a hunch — and following it.

He checked that Riley had water, then scooped the Sprite's keys off the galley counter and, leaving a light on, locked the boat and left.

TRICKY ENOUGH DRIVING around here during the day, he had pretty much avoided any extended night driving where the looming hedges could turn into black walls that swallowed an oncoming car's headlights.

Ignition on, the Sprite's engine gave off a deep, sweet roar — one of the things he loved about it. It required a lot of TLC but — like most demanding things in life — it was worth it.

Headlights on, he pulled onto the small road that led away from his boat's mooring, and drove, even more slowly than normal, towards the village, thinking through the details of his hunch.

Sarah's friend had come to the village. And though the police seemed to think she came by car, there was no car registered to her. So, if she came in a car and met someone here then *that* car — a rental maybe, or a car she borrowed from someone yet unknown — had to be somewhere.

The police would probably find it. Even without any top-shelf detecting skills, if it was within ten miles of Cherringham, they'd eventually locate it.

But he wanted to find it first.

Could be a long night, he thought.

HE DROVE SLOWLY through the village, looking at the restaurants, the unlit shops, people doing late-night shopping at Cherringham's only convenience store.

If you wanted to put a car somewhere no one would notice it, where exactly would that be?

Jack had seen people do that every week since he came here.

People who'd drop their cars in a car park, and train into London.

Lot of unnoticed cars there.

But how could he tell which one might be Sammi's?

He literally didn't have a clue about that.

HE WAS COMING up to the car park but then saw, parked across the street in front of the Railway Arms, a police car.

An officer stood outside talking to a man who, even at this distance, Jack could see was wavering in the wind.

Couldn't go into the car park now. Not with a cop right there.

He'd have to do another loop, though to a sharp-eyed cop even that would look suspicious.

Might help if I had a less recognizable vehicle, he thought. Not too many of these throaty little sports cars running around.

Need some generic Ford. Something so bland as to be unnoticed.

He drove past the pub, giving the scene with the cop and the drunk only a quick glance.

And he left the warm glow of the village, lit up at night, for the dark road that headed west, to the hills past Cherringham.

LOOPING BACK, LIKE a fighter plane on a strafing run, he drove down the street that led to the pub, hoping that Cherringham's finest had cleared up whatever trouble had been there.

The big car park was just across the way. It was large because the train station was close by.

He took a breath, and then saw the lit sign of the Railway Arms.

The police car was gone.

He slowed, put on his turn indicator, and, just as he entered the car park, he killed his lights.

JACK CRUISED UP and down the aisles of cars, thinking, wondering… what am I looking for?

Sometimes when you follow a hunch, he thought, you have to hope something will just leap out at you.

He passed the pay meters at one end. You could buy a few hours or a day's parking. Nothing more. So this was strictly for commuters.

Okay. That might be useful.

He turned down the next aisle of cars, his eyes adjusting to the darkness as he kept the sports car to crawl. Looking, left, then right, searching for a sign from the automobile gods.

Something. *Anything.*

Then he came abreast of a car that had papers stuck to its windshield by the wipers, flapping in the gentle evening wind.

Parking tickets.

For someone who left the car there and hasn't come back in two or three days.

He stopped the Sprite. Across from the suspect car — a boxy Honda of some kind — he spotted an empty parking space.

And he pulled in thinking: *I haven't been this excited in a long time.*

JACK LOOKED AROUND to make sure no one was watching, and then popped open the tiny boot of the Sprite.

He walked to the back and pulled out a thin metal rod.

Been a while. But this should be just like riding a bike.

He closed the boot as slowly and quietly as possible.

While he may have once been a decorated member of the NYPD, Jack imagined that breaking into a car would still be viewed by the locals as a crime.

He walked over to the Honda, the tickets still blowing in the wind. Four of them, so the car could have been there three days, which matched perfectly the time Sammi arrived in Cherringham.

He leaned closer to the car, and hiding the shiny piece of metal with his body, he made the metal strip slip between the window pane and the door slot. He looked into the car to check for any theft alarm but didn't see the glowing red light.

Okay, he thought.

So when I pop this, I won't have an alarm screaming through the car park, waking the dead and those glued to their stools in the pub.

Then: *Here goes.*

With a quick motion he slid the metal bar down and fished around to find where the inside lock connected to the manual one on the inside of the door.

Despite his confidence that he could do this, it wasn't going well.

He shook his head, wondering how long before the cop car did another loop, maybe came in here.

That would end any detecting.

He also had the thought… *what am I really doing?*

I'm done with all this, aren't I?

But even as he had those thoughts, with a gentle summer breeze blowing through the trees creating a soft rustling noise, the village at night so quiet, so sleepy, he hit something.

Something stopped the bar and — if the car door was organized the way ninety-nine per cent of them were — he should be able to bend the bar, and from the inside trigger the door latch to open.

And then — an open sesame moment — he watched the door lock pop up.

The car that had been parked here since Monday, gathering parking tickets from the attendant but still so far under the radar of the local cops, was now unlocked.

And as fast as he could he popped open the door, and slid into the Honda.

THE CAR LOOKED and smelled new. No whiff of marijuana, no tell-tale powder on the seats.

A rental, a friend's car? Now inside, still no way for Jack to tell. And he didn't find any slips of paper, a petrol receipt, directions to

Cherringham, anything that told him who may have been driving.

Could be just some commuter who didn't care if he collected a few tickets while in London.

He reached down to the side-door compartment, which was empty and then over to the glove compartment, which also was pristine save for the car's manual in a leatherette cover.

The great NYC detective strikes out, he thought.

And he had such high hopes for his idea.

He could check plates but that would take a few calls — and favours — to some London friends on the job. And the more time that went on, the colder this whole thing got.

So cold, he had to wonder if it was too late?

He reached under the driver's seat, then the passenger's seat. Nothing.

He guessed that if he looked in the boot it would have been equally immaculate.

He turned and looked at the back seat which, even in the darkness, with just a bit of milky light from a distant car park lamp, he could see was empty.

Time to give this up, he thought.

One more thing.

And he twisted around so he could turn and lean into the back. And then, looking down, he checked the floor of the car in front of those seats.

And there, just behind the driver's seat was a lump of some kind.

Jack reached down for it, stretching more, delivering a spike of pain to his side muscles.

Not as limber as I used to be.

He reached for the object, just out of reach. A bit more of a painful stretch, and his fingers closed on the object, pulling it up off the floor.

MURDER ON THAMES

And even before he got a good look at it, he knew what it was.

A phone. Hidden back there.

Maybe left behind on purpose? Maybe dropped, wobbly after mixing drugs and drinks??

Jack knew how useful phones could be.

He slid it into his shirt pocket — this was not the place to make it spring to life.

He looked around the car park which was still deserted but then heard a train in the distance. The late commuters would be coming here soon.

He grabbed the metal rod and opened the door, keeping low so that his head didn't loom over the small Honda.

And then, crouching, he walked back to his Sprite, which was now looking even more absurdly small, especially when he wanted it to be hidden, unobserved.

The train was pulling into the station.

He fished out his keys, started the car — always a throw of the dice with a temperamental sports car — and, with a rumble, he started to back away, lights still off.

Slowly he moved past the Honda, looping around to the entrance across from the pub as the train now screeched to a halt in the station behind him.

People hit the stairs from the platform, up to the walkway to the car park.

Jack got to the entrance, turned on his lights and, forcing himself to drive slowly when all he wanted to do was step on it, he pulled away.

16.

THE LAST TEXTS

SARAH SAT AT the kitchen table with the TV on but muted so she couldn't hear explosive laughter from whomever the chat show host found so amazingly funny.

She hoped that Jack would call, curious about what he was up to that he couldn't tell her about and also wanting to share what Lou Tidewell said.

She had this feeling, now stronger than ever, that they were close to *something*. And that while her friend might be dead, Sarah would do all she could to find out how it happened.

Her phone sat on the counter, quiet. Maybe a glass of Pinot Noir, she thought? And just as that idea seemed so appealing, the phone vibrated and she snatched it up.

"Hello?"

Jack.

"Look. Sarah, I found something. Love to show you."

"Right. When? Tomorrow?"

He hesitated. "Can you get away for a bit now?"

It was late and Daniel and Chloe were both in their rooms. She had to remember that she was a mum.

I can't lose sight of that, she thought.

"I don't know, Jack."

Which is when Chloe walked into the kitchen, her face set. Still a hint of disapproval there. Sarah smiled at her.

"Can I ring you right back?"

"Sure. I'll wait."

Sarah killed the call, and then turned to face her daughter.

"THAT *HIM?* The American?"

Sarah nodded. "You say that like he's an invader."

Chloe's non-response showed that was exactly what she *did* think.

"Chloe, I wonder... He called, said he found out something. About my friend, Sammi. Think you could keep an eye on Daniel for a while?"

"Mum. He's nearly eleven!"

Sarah nodded. "I'd feel better knowing you were, you know, in charge. I'll be quick."

Her daughter seemed to hold onto her stern pose for a few more moments then nodded. "Sure."

"You're a star, Chloe. Be back before your bedtimes."

Chloe nodded again, then turned, walked away.

Sarah hesitated a moment, thinking that maybe she needed to talk to her daughter about what happened to their lives. She was growing up so fast.

And not for the first time Sarah thought how hard this was to do, all alone.

Then she touched her phone's screen to call Jack back.

THE SPRITE RUMBLED outside the house like a big cat in the zoo.

She imagined her neighbours, twitching behind their curtains, wondering, *whatever* is that Sarah Edwards up to? In a village like this, your business was everybody's business.

She opened the passenger door and slid in.

"Trouble getting a pass?"

Sarah turned to Jack. "Don't think my daughter likes you Yanks."

Jack tilted his head, as if confused. "She doesn't think that we're…"

Sarah shook her head.

"No. I mean, I told her what we're doing. But you know — teenage girls."

Jack smiled. "Had one of those myself."

Sarah noted that comment, reminded suddenly of how little she knew about Jack and his past. But now wasn't the time for family histories.

He pulled away from the house.

"Where we going?" she asked.

"Just going to drive around while I tell you what I found."

"Important?"

"Could be…"

JACK TURNED OFF the engine. They'd pulled in at Cherringham's only twenty-four-hour petrol station up on the main road just outside the village.

The place was brightly lit but empty. Sarah could see the guy at the till, drinking coffee, feet up, watching them parked in the tyre pressure bay.

In the shadows.

What do we look like? she thought.

Jack handed her the phone.

"What's this?"

"Found it. In a car with a lot of tickets on it. In the station car park."

"You broke in?"

His eyes straight on the road, he nodded.

"Plausible deniability?"

"Exactly. Now look at the texts."

The phone was a cheap pay-as-you-go flip phone, basic, easy to operate. Disposable.

Sarah opened up the text history. There was a string of texts — from just one number. She scrolled through them quickly.

"Whoa. They've been sent every few minutes — it's a conversation. 'Don't do anything stupid.' 'You owe me.' 'We have to talk first.' 'Don't threaten me.'"

"See the last one?"

"'Meet me by the weir'," she said. "'Now'."

"Sent by the other person on the evening she died."

Sarah looked at Jack, a shaft of neon light from inside the garage making his face look gaunt and serious.

"Well, this proves it, doesn't it?" she said.

But Jack shook his head. "Proves nothing — except that somebody who parked in the station car park had an argument. And wanted to meet someone at the river. Earlier that evening. A lot earlier. Doesn't quite fit."

"But it's got to be Sammi," said Sarah. "Lou Tidewell told me that Sammi was dressed up to the nines. Dressed for a date…"

"That so?"

On impulse, she took out her phone and tapped in the number on the texts. But it didn't even ring.

"No answer. Nothing, not even voicemail," she said.

"Not surprised," said Jack. "He'll have got rid of the phone long ago."

"So what now?" said Sarah. "Do we talk to the police?"

"And tell them what?" said Jack.

"We've got the texts."

"Okay. But you got to see this from the cops' point of view, Sarah. It might not be Sammi's phone. And if it is — all it proves is she was having a text argument with a boyfriend. We still don't have proof she was murdered."

Sarah looked around at the dismal, empty petrol station. Every now and then a car raced past in a blur of light down the main road and away from the village.

This was so frustrating. They were getting nowhere. She looked at her watch — nearly ten.

"I've got to get back."

"Sure."

Jack shrugged and started up the little sports car.

As they drove across the brightly lit forecourt towards the main road, Sarah felt the cashier's eyes on them.

And suddenly she felt like a complete fool. What was she doing driving around at night with some American guy — some *old* guy as Chloe called him — a guy she hardly knew, pretending to be a detective on a case?

In the darkness of the car, she cringed to herself. No wonder Chloe was getting at her. She was being an idiot.

Sammi had died. Committed suicide. And she — Sarah — was a single mother of two with responsibilities, and a company and the beginnings of a new life here that might just about bring her back some self-respect and security and peace.

She was a web-designer. Not a cop.

"Hey. You okay?" said Jack, as they turned into the high street.

"Yeah, yeah. It's late and I need to get Daniel to bed. Left on his own, he'll stay up all night with his games."

"Sure. I'll have you home in a couple of minutes," said Jack.

Sarah's phone pinged. She opened it up — a text from Chloe. No words — just a question mark. And Sarah knew just what that one symbol meant.

Where are you? What are you doing? What the hell's going on, mum?

And worse — it had been sent half an hour ago. The mobile phone coverage round Cherringham was so sparse — sometimes messages could take hours to get through.

Sarah felt guilty. Chloe must have been sitting around all this time waiting for a text back, worrying.

When were they ever going to get a decent mobile coverage round here?

Hang on a minute …

"Jack — give me the phone again, would you?"

Without taking his eyes off the road, Jack reached into his jacket pocket, took out the phone and handed it to her.

She turned it on and pulled up the texts.

"This text telling her to meet," she said. "Sent at nine o'clock."

"Uh-huh."

"But go to the sent texts — and the reply doesn't go off till 11.58."

"So? Whoever sent it took their time to reply."

"No," said Sarah. "That's it! I think the reply was sent straight away. It's just that the first text took a long time to arrive. It happens here a lot."

"So whoever sent it was waiting by the weir that whole time?"

"Makes sense, doesn't it," said Sarah, her head clear again. "And if it was Gordon Williams…"

"In the big flashy SUV…"

"Exactly," said Sarah. "Somebody might have seen him."

They pulled up outside Sarah's house. She could see the lights in the house were still all on — Daniel and Chloe on the sofa no doubt watching some dubious film.

"Talk in the morning, huh?" said Jack, as she climbed out.

"I'll call you," said Sarah. "Daniel's got a cricket match — and it's my turn to do the ferrying. So it'll be midday."

"No problem. I'd offer to come with you, but cricket's one of those mysteries that's going to stay that way," said Jack. "And Sarah…"

"Yeah?"

"You're doing the right thing here, you know. Sammi was your friend. And nobody else is looking out for her."

Sarah nodded.

"Talk tomorrow," she said.

Jack drove off with a quick wave. She took out her key and headed for the front door. She hadn't felt like this since she was a teenager sneaking back into her parents' house after midnight.

17.

IT'S ALL ABOUT THE TIMING

JACK WAS UP early. He had a lot to do.

First, his usual walk up the river and back with Riley then a shower, breakfast on deck — bacon, eggs over easy — and finally a list of phone calls to some old friends.

Favours to call in. You don't work thirty years in homicide without getting to know cops around the globe. And, in Jack's case, making one or two lasting friendships too.

With a few wheels nicely set in motion, he left Riley a couple of treats, locked up the boat and headed off down the towpath toward Cherringham Toll Bridge.

JACK TAPPED ON the little glass window of the toll bridge booth. Inside he could see the two old ladies sitting at a table drinking tea and chatting.

They both looked up at him, clearly irritated. One of them gestured to an old clock on the wall, mouthed 'we're closed', then they both muttered and went back to their teas.

Jack stepped back and sighed.

Yes, he knew it was 7.45. And he knew the two women didn't start charging traffic on the bridge until 8 o'clock but that was exactly why he'd timed his walk to get here early.

On either side of the booth the traffic was whizzing by in and out of Cherringham — early birds grateful not to have to pay twenty pence a trip and get caught up in a queue.

He tapped again on the window and put on his cheesiest smile. The women stopped talking again and stared at him. He looked from one to the other. Grey hair tightly bound in buns, over-large glasses, buttoned up blouses and cardigans — these two were the matching Great Aunts from Hell.

And then he realized.

My God — they're twins…

Slowly, laboriously, the twin with the meaner face put down her dainty little cup of tea, came over to the window and slid it open.

"If you've got a complaint, you'll have to make it to the council," she said, preparing to close the window again.

"No, no, it's not a complaint," Jack replied. "I'm…"

She hesitated. Maybe it was his accent?

"Well, we're shut," she said.

"I need your help."

"Phone box down the road — we're not a garage you know," she said crisply.

"What is it, Joan, is it *trouble?*" said the other twin, rising from the table and peering at Jack. Her glasses caught the early morning sun, turning to blank discs. This was becoming a horror movie, thought Jack.

"Please ladies, I really am sorry for disturbing you. I just need to ask you some questions,"

"Oh? Are you a policeman then?"

"Well — I used to be," said Jack. "But I'm not officially

anymore."

"And American too, huh?"

"Yank is it?"

"Guilty," Jack said with what he hoped was a winning smile.

The two women were now together at the window, both peering at Jack like he was some kind of specimen.

"New Yorker from the sound of it."

"New York's finest," said the second woman. "Are you?"

"Oh, be quiet Jen," said Joan without taking her eyes off Jack. "What kind of questions?"

They seemed to soften a bit.

Something about this interested them.

"About the girl who died in the river," he said.

"Murder case is it now?" said Jen.

"Doesn't surprise me," said Joan.

"Or me," said Jen.

"You'd better come in," said Joan.

And with that she slid the little window shut and the two women disappeared into the darkness of the hut.

Jack waited for a second, confused by the simultaneous invitation and rejection. Then the two women appeared at the other end of the hut.

"Well, come on then, we haven't got all day," said Joan.

"We start at eight you know," said Jen, looking at her watch. "You've got three minutes."

JACK WAS GLAD he'd started the day with a long walk. Sitting in a comfy chair at the back of the hut, he'd eaten enough cake and biscuits for a week, and still the two old ladies were finding more for him to try…

94

'Just a teeny mouthful, won't do any harm Joan, will it?'

'Needs feeding up, that's what I think, Jen.'

From the moment he'd suggested that Sammi's death was suspicious he'd gone from being irritating intruder to honoured guest.

It turned out that Jen and Joan were crime fans. The little hut was a library — every wall was lined with shelves, each filled with crime fiction. There was everything from mysteries to leather-bound editions of Sherlock Holmes, from police procedurals to serial killer bios, all of which meant that his little request had gone down a storm.

Could they let him see the CCTV footage from the toll booth for Monday evening?

Could they just!

While Jen racked up the twenty pence tolls every ten seconds, Joan helped him search the stored footage frame by frame. And when Jen's half hour at the coal-face was up, Joan took over and Jen joined him at the little CCTV monitor, loading discs.

Even though the toll booth was only open from eight in the morning to eight at night, the CCTV cameras ran 24/7: late-night revellers from the village had a tendency to speed across the bridge and more than once in the past they'd ended up smack in the middle of the toll booth.

So Jen and Joan had installed the cameras to make sure the insurance always paid out but although the cameras were always on, the lenses weren't often cleaned. Jack realized pretty swiftly that although the cars might be visible, the plates and drivers were blurred behind months of grime.

Nevertheless, he knew this was worth doing. There were no other CCTV cameras in the village — and this was the main route in and out.

It was also the nearest road to the weir: if the killer came this way, he must have passed by the cameras.

He took another bite of lemon meringue pie.

"Pop the next disc in, Joan," he said. "Where are we now?"

"Six fifty-eight," said Joan. "Just another six hours to go."

"One more cup in that pot, you reckon, Jen?" said Jack. "I must say, you ladies know how to throw a tea-party."

Busting drug dealers in Manhattan was never this cosy, thought Jack.

I wish…

18.

STICKY WICKET

SARAH LINED UP the plastic cups on the tray and carefully poured orange juice into each one.

Cherringham's Under Twelves were fielding and when the weather was hot like this everyone needed a drink break. Today was her turn to do refreshments.

Daniel's team used the Cherringham Cricket Club pitch just on the edge of the village. It wasn't anything special — just a little hut with a few changing rooms and a kitchen, and a stack of plastic chairs for the parents and the batting team to sit and watch the game.

She carried the tray of drinks over to the knot of players standing together in the shade of a line of oak trees. She nodded to Daniel and he gave her only the slightest of nods back. Barely a flicker of recognition. Sarah knew the rules. This wasn't the time to chat. Not while he was with his mates, all boys together. Bad enough that mum was bringing the drinks over.

She'd learned to get over that — or at least to *appear* not to mind. But it still made her heart jump a little.

One of the dads — Graham — came over to help her out with the drinks. Like her, Graham was a single parent, though in his case he'd lost his wife to cancer a year ago. Sarah had vaguely known them both, but they'd never really been what she'd call friends.

Graham spent most of these cricket mornings trying to chat to her.

"Cherringham's single mums and dads society — that's us Sarah!" he'd say with a cheesy grin.

"Yep, that's us, Graham!" she'd say back. She just couldn't be so heartless as to say the truth — you're so very sweet Graham, but please, no, don't even *think* about it. But there he was like a little puppy, every weekend.

Bring on the football season. His little Archy was no footballer, thank God.

Graham walked her back to the cricket hut, while the boys went back onto the field.

"I hear you're telling everyone that girl was murdered, Sarah," he said.

"What?" said Sarah, momentarily thrown.

"Brian in the pub — he told me you'd hired a private detective. Some hard-nosed American."

"Oh really?" she said, recovering. "Well, you can tell Brian he's wrong. And if I need someone hard-boiled, he'll be first on my list."

"So it's not true then?"

"Graham — I have not hired a private detective. Okay? And to be honest, I'd really appreciate it if you didn't spread that kind of gossip around."

She saw Graham flinch and realized straight away that she'd hurt him.

"Graham, sorry, I didn't — that came out all wrong, what I meant was—"

"It's fine, Sarah. Not a problem," he interrupted. "Look, they said they might need a hand doing the scoring, so I'll just pop over and help them out. Catch you later."

Sarah watched him walk off, his shoulders slumped.

Terrific. Not only do I piss my kids off, I also start laying into the most inoffensive guy in the whole village.

What am I doing?

From the car park came the throaty roar of a car. A sports car.

Jack's car.

She looked across. This was all she needed.

She watched as he climbed out of his little car and took his bearings. When he saw the pitch and the little group of spectators, he headed straight for them.

Sarah folded her arms and waited for him to reach her. Out of the corner of her eye she could sense the other parents had gone quiet and were watching this interesting new arrival onto the Cherringham children's cricket scene.

What was he doing here?

She'd told him she'd call him — hadn't she? This was just getting beyond a joke. He had no right to just turn up on... on a Saturday!

"Hey Sarah," he said, all cheery. "How's it going?"

Sarah kept her cool.

"Hi, Jack," she said. "I didn't expect to see you this morning."

She watched as Jack sized up the situation, turning to a little group of staring parents, giving them a nod.

He did stand out...

Then he turned back to Sarah.

"We winning? As if I'd know, huh?"

He laughed, and then she led him away from the chairs and over to the relative safety of the empty hut.

"I said I'd call you Jack — you didn't need to come up here," she said. "How did you find us anyway? Of course, you're a cop — how could I forget?"

"Whoa," he said. "Sarah — I know what you said. But I also know this couldn't wait — okay?"

"Go on," she said, in no mood to forgive him for breaking into her family time. Especially when she'd been doing such a good job of wrecking it herself…

"So listen. I went through the CCTV footage down at the toll booth."

For a second Sarah forgot how angry she was.

"You did *what?*" she said. "With or without the Buckland girls' permission?"

"Those two pussycats?" he said. "They even gave me one of their secret recipes."

"Let me guess — eye of newt quiche?"

"Hey, don't mock. I think they just helped us crack this case."

"Seriously?" said Sarah.

Jack nodded. He took out his smartphone and held it out.

"We went through Monday's CCTV — the whole evening, from five that afternoon to one the next morning," he said. "And guess what we found."

He scrolled through the photos on the phone.

"Nice one of Riley," she said.

"Huh? No — this one."

Sarah looked at the screen.

"These are just photos of their screen. The quality's not great — but that's not actually the phone's fault, it's the dirty cameras they've got running there. Anyway — you see the two frames. First one — just after eight in the evening."

Sarah peered at the fuzzy image.

"Range Rover Sport."

"Correct," said Jack. "And the plate is Williams'. Now look at this — one in the morning, going the other way."

Sarah stared hard. It was the same car — no doubt about it.

"But do you see the difference between the cars?"

Sarah flicked the images back and forth. And suddenly understood.

"It's clean — shiny, even — in this one at eight. I can see that clear enough, even with a dirty camera. But coming back — it's covered in mud!"

"Remember when we went and saw him, the kid was cleaning it?" said Jack.

"That's right," she said. "So Williams lied about being in London?"

"That's possible," said Jack. "At the very least — we got enough reason to go back to him and ask him. Don't you think?"

"Shame we can't see who's driving," she said.

"Yeah. Back home, we had guys could enhance a picture like this, get a clear image."

"Hang on. That's not a problem," said Sarah. "I know people who can do that."

"You do?"

"Don't sound so surprised. This is my world — remember? Tech? Just text me the photos and I'll get someone on it."

"Terrific," said Jack. "So what are we waiting for? Let's go talk to Mr Williams, shall we?"

"It's going to have to wait, Jack," said Sarah. "We've got at least an hour's play here."

"Oh," said Jack.

"So unless you want to watch the cricket — maybe we revert to the original plan, and I call you when I'm ready?"

Jack shrugged.

"Sure," he said, turning to head back to his car. "I don't think me and cricket are quite ready for each other yet. Know what I mean?"

Sarah watched him go. And felt bad that she'd taken it out on him. Luckily, he didn't seem to notice.

No, she thought — *he notices. He just chooses not to be bothered by it.*

19.

KEEP IT IN THE FAMILY

JACK CAREFULLY WOUND the silver wire round and round the hook then snipped it off with his pliers.

All he had to do now was go back over the length with thread, then varnish the whole thing — and he'd have his first fishing fly.

He could have just bought a ready-made fly from the local tackle shop — but this was way more satisfying. He sat back in his office chair, took a sip of coffee, gave his eyes a rest.

Not by nature a hobbyist, he was beginning to value this new craft: it gave him time to think things through.

This case for instance. Though it seemed they were on the very edge of cracking it — the thing was full of holes too.

There was no shortage of suspects — or motives. Sammi's dad clearly hated her. But would he kill her just for coming home, maybe asking for more money? Robbo had a violent temper — and it was the kind that Jack had often seen spill over into murder. But Robbo didn't smell guilty to Jack.

If Williams was Sammi's lover — and she'd turned on him, threatened to tell his wife, perhaps — then he certainly had a strong motive for getting rid of her. Jack hadn't liked him, but over the years he'd learned not to let that cloud his judgement. And, so far, they didn't have much to connect him to Sammi apart from the car being seen near the weir.

It came down to one thing — was Williams the sugar daddy?

His phone rang. He looked at the number on the screen. London.

Was this call going to give him the answer?

JACK SAT PATIENTLY in the front passenger seat of Sarah's car while she dropped the last boy off.

"You got everything, Harry?" said Sarah. "Well played, love. Say hi to your mum for me, won't you?"

Jack leaned round as Harry pulled his cricket bag off the back seat and slammed the car door.

"Bye Mrs Edwards. Thanks for the lift."

Sarah waited until the boy had gone into his house, then pulled out into the traffic and picked up speed.

"Well, that was a mighty interesting little tour of the neighbourhood," said Jack.

"Sorry Jack, didn't have any choice," said Sarah. "Some of the parents have to leave early so it's just luck of the draw who ends up taking the players home. And today I got short straw."

"No problem."

"Saturdays get kind of busy."

"I can see."

"So, what's the plan?" said Sarah.

"I think we put the squeeze on Mr Williams. See if he bends a little."

"Didn't we already do that? What's different now?"

"Ah well," said Jack. "I'll tell you what's different. Pal of mine in your Fraud Squad in London did a little digging into some phone payments for me last night. And he's come back with some very interesting information."

"Isn't that illegal?" said Sarah.

"I prefer the word 'questionable'. Bit of a grey area. Especially these days."

"So go on — tell me what he said."

"Our mystery texter: 'meet me by the weir'. Well *that* phone was topped up using a Barclay's credit card registered to a certain Mr Gordon Williams, address Imperial House, Lower Runstead. He also confirmed that the phone from the car was registered to Sammi."

"Wow. So isn't that what we need? The proof?"

Jack shrugged.

"It's good. Very good, since it proves Williams and Sammi were communicating with each other on the night she died. It proves he suggested meeting her by the weir."

"But it doesn't prove he killed her?" said Sarah.

"Correct. It doesn't even prove they met."

"So why are we going to talk to him?"

"Because he lied to us. And when people get caught out in a lie, they tend to offer up other stuff too. You just never know what."

"We'll soon find out," said Sarah, as she stopped the car at the entrance to Imperial House.

JACK WATCHED SARAH as she pressed the gate buzzer again.

"Nothing?" he said.

Sarah shrugged.

"It's a trade-off," said Jack. "You want to surprise the bad guys — and sometimes the bad guys aren't in."

"Or they're about to arrive home ..." said Sarah, gesturing

behind them.

Jack turned in his seat. A silver Mercedes glided next to them and stopped. At the wheel was Gordon Williams.

He slid the window down.

"You again?" he said. "What now?" Then: "You'd better follow me."

Ahead of them, the automatic gates opened and the Mercedes purred away up the drive towards the house.

Sarah let off the brake and they followed.

"You thinking what I'm thinking?" said Sarah.

"Yep."

"We kinda assumed that was his only car, didn't we?"

"We did," said Jack. "Seems I'm a little out of practice."

When they reached the front of the house, Williams had already parked the car and was heading into the house.

Sarah followed his lead.

"Guess we're invited," said Jack and he strolled through the front door, Sarah right behind.

JACK LOOKED AROUND the grand hallway. Two semi-circular staircases rose ahead, lit by a tall stained-glass window. A massive chandelier hung from the high ceiling above the gleaming parquet floor.

Williams was checking post laid out on a beautiful carved table.

He turned and faced them.

"This is going to be quick — all right? And when we're finished, I don't expect to see either of you again. Am I clear?"

"Mr Williams, I think that depends on what you're going to tell us," said Jack.

Jack saw Williams take a quick look around, as if checking

nobody else was in earshot.

"Okay. Right. When you came the other day — I wasn't entirely accurate. There was something going on between me and Sammi. Not an affair — God forbid. But... an arrangement. She liked the high life, did Sammi. But she never earned enough to afford it. So we'd go out together, when I was in London."

"So you were sleeping with her, Mr Williams?" said Sarah.

"Er, yes. Obviously."

"*Obviously*," said Sarah.

"Anyway that wasn't good enough for Sammi. She wanted cash too. I said no — I didn't use prostitutes. That seemed to upset her."

"I'm sure it did, Mr Williams," said Jack, straight-faced.

"So she tried to blackmail me. Said she'd tell my wife. Tell the board of Imperial too."

"That's terrible," said Sarah.

Jack watched her and remembered how she'd asked him to stop her from hitting Robbo that time. He could see her fists clenching, in just the same way.

"Too right it was terrible. Anyway — I tried to reason with her. But she wouldn't listen."

"So that's why you sent her the texts," said Jack, just wanting to tease him along.

Like trout fishing, he suddenly thought. And here's the fly — the phone...

But Williams didn't jump for it.

"What? What texts?" he said.

"The ones you sent her on the day she died," said Jack.

He was aware of Sarah's eyes on him. And aware too that Williams' surprise seemed genuine.

"I didn't send her any texts," said Williams.

Jack took out the phone he'd found in the car, and scrolled to the texts. He showed it to Williams.

"Really? How about these?" said Jack.

Williams peered at the texts and scrolled back through them.

"The ones from a couple of weeks ago — yes, I sent those. But not these. I've never seen these before."

"That's rather convenient, isn't it, Mr Williams?" said Sarah.

"Convenient and *true*. As it happens, I lost my phone about ten days ago, the one I used to text Sammi. Bloody good thing I thought at the time — stopped her bothering me."

"So who sent the texts?" said Jack.

"How the hell should I know?" said Williams. "Presumably whoever found my phone. Or stole it."

Jack looked at Williams and then at Sarah. He was thinking fast. But whichever way he cut this, Williams was suddenly looking innocent.

Innocent of murder at least.

So the texter could still be the killer — but who was it? Someone who worked with Williams? And why? Jealousy?

A horn sounded outside. Jack saw Williams check his watch.

"Interview over. I'm late. And you're leaving."

He grabbed a jacket slung over the back of a chair and took them to the front door.

Jack felt himself being propelled — albeit politely — through the front door and out into the gravel parking area in front of the house.

Behind him he could hear Sarah's phone ping with a message.

Outside in the bright sunshine, the black Range Rover Sport was waiting. Standing next to it was Kaz in black skinny suit and expensive white shirt.

"Come on, Dad," said the young man, climbing into the driver seat. "We're late already."

Williams walked around the car to get into the passenger seat.

Jack's brain went into overdrive.

The son was going to drive.

The *son* had been on the cruise with Williams and his wife.

The son had been cleaning mud off the car.

The son had access to his father's phone.

Jack looked to Sarah for help, but she seemed pre-occupied by her phone.

And before Jack could re-arrange the whole case in his head, she stepped in front of him and leaned down to the driver window.

"You heading into Cherringham?" she said, smiling at Kaz.

"Yeah."

Jack frowned — what the hell was Sarah doing?

"Let me guess," she said. "You're going to the Operatic Society?"

"Right," said Kaz. "Mum's singing."

"Should be good," said Sarah. "I'm supposed to be there, too. Gosh, it starts in half an hour."

Williams leaned across his son to the driver window.

"So if you don't mind — we need to go now."

Jack saw Sarah smile at Kaz. He smiled back, obviously trying to make up for his father's rude tone.

"Mum's singing the lead," he said proudly.

"Let me guess," said Sarah. "Soprano?"

"That's right," said Kaz. "How did you know?"

Jack heard Sarah's tone, flat.

"Oh, my mother's in the choir too."

Right, Jack thought, and Sarah's mum had mentioned that their lead soprano had missed the rehearsal.

The night Sammi died.

Williams tapped his son on the knee and motioned impatiently

MURDER ON THAMES

to him to get going.

"The gate will stay open for a couple of minutes," said Williams through the open window. "You'd better be quick."

And with that the Range Rover pulled away, spinning gravel.

Jack watched it go. He wasn't surprised when Sarah held out her phone to him and flicked open the photos.

He looked down at the enhanced CCTV shots from the Cherringham Toll Bridge.

Driving into Cherringham in the black Range Rover Sport, then driving out again four hours later …

Maureen Williams.

The soprano who'd called in sick for rehearsal on the night that Sammi died. Cherringham's own 'Nedda', who cheats on her clown-husband, 'Canio'.

Maureen Williams.

The murderer.

20.

IT AIN'T OVER 'TIL...

JACK STOOD BESIDE Sarah at the back of the small village-hall theatre, all the seats taken as the grisly tale of infidelity and murder played out on stage.

Pagliacci was one of Jack's favourites, and he thought that — for a small village with a chamber-sized orchestra — the Cherringham Operatic Society wasn't doing too badly.

And now, as Leoncavallo's lone masterpiece neared its bloody climax, the audience sat up straight, attention focused, as everyone knew what must inevitably happen on stage.

He looked at Sarah.

If she hadn't seen this before, she was in for a shock.

On stage, Canio, the leader of the roving troupe of players, sang full out, a bit of a wobbly tenor but chilling as he demanded the 'name' — the name of his wife Nedda's lover.

Now, in the opera's last moments, Nedda continued to protest her innocence, refusing to name names as Canio became more and more incensed, the tenor's pitch even more shaky as it gained — Jack had to admit — a gripping dramatic power.

Nedda — terrified by her husband's madness — started to flee, only to be grabbed by Canio, his hands tight around her neck, before he pulled out a knife and stabbed his cheating wife.

The singer playing Nedda's lover began rushing to stop Canio — only to be stabbed himself.

Ah, Opera. The body count growing, Jack thought.

Canio took the knife from where it was embedded in the lover's body and, arms down and tears in his eyes, spoke the last, always chilling words of the opera.

"La commedia è finite!"

And the full-house of Cherringham residents erupted into applause, unaware that the real drama was only moments away.

Jack felt Sarah touch his shoulder and, with a nod, indicated that they should wait outside.

SARAH STOOD BETWEEN Jack and Alan, whom she had called as they went to the theatre, filling him in quickly in the car.

He'd had a lot of questions, and was more than dubious, but in the end, he had to recognize that they had solved the mystery of Sammi's death.

When the performance ended Sarah had given her mum hugs and congratulations, then packed her off with her dad, Daniel and Chloe to the Spotted Pig where she'd meet them later for dinner.

Just got something important to sort out, Mum, won't be long…

Now, with the rest of the audience gone, retiring to other pubs and restaurants, the three of them stood there in Cherringham's old square, awaiting one singer.

Maureen Williams. The cheating Nedda, unaware of what awaited her outside.

Funny, Sarah thought, *how in one moment your life can change. Just as it did for Sammi.*

Gordon Williams opened the door of the hall, followed by his wife and son, all smiles, bubbly with the adrenaline rush of the successful show.

But Gordy stopped upon seeing Sarah and Jack standing with Alan, in uniform, seemingly waiting for them. Alan had agreed to let Sarah talk first.

You did the work, he had said.

Amazing. Not defensive at all.

But it was Gordon who spoke first.

"What? You again?"

With a nod, Jack indicated Sarah should take the lead.

And she ignored the husband. "Mrs Williams. We found Sammi's phone. With the messages."

Sarah held it up.

"And there were photos from the toll bridge CCTV. The cameras saw you. The night Sammi died."

The woman's eyes turned even wider than when her clown-husband had his stage knife raised to her.

"You found your husband's phone and realized what had been going on," Sarah continued. "So you decided to text Sammi."

Maureen Williams started shaking her head, horrified.

Gordon turned to her. "Say nothing, my dear. Our solicitor will—"

But, Sarah guessed, Maureen Williams had long ago stopped listening to her cheating husband.

She turned on him. "*You.* And your London whores. As if I didn't know."

Sarah shot a glance at Jack, wondering: *is this how it's supposed to go?*

"Maureen, darling, you must stop—"

"I must? You would have let that little bitch destroy us, destroy our family. Such a stupid girl, but you..." she gave a humourless laugh. "You like them that way."

Sarah looked at Kaz, his face rigid, and she felt the worst for him, having to watch this scene.

Alan cleared his throat. "Mrs Williams, I'm afraid—"

But Maureen Williams — the woman scorned — wasn't quite done. "She was so easily pushed into the water. Just skin and bones in her glittery frock, dressed so prettily for you! So stupid and easy to hold under."

Sarah felt her stomach tighten. How do real police detectives do this? She wanted to take her hand, now tightened into a fist, and slam it hard into the woman who had killed her friend.

Alan took a step closer. A hand to Maureen Williams's arm.

"Alan, I'm sure there's no need..." Gordon sputtered, sounding desperate.

But there was. Murder was murder, even here in this tight-knit world of Cherringham.

"Mrs Williams, I'm afraid you'll have to come with me."

And with those words, the policeman slowly, almost gently, started to lead her away.

Sarah wanted to say something more to the man who was really responsible for this — Gordon Williams.

But then she felt a hand on her elbow.

Jack.

Leaning close he said, "We'd best go, Sarah." He took a breath. The air was cool for a summer's night. "We're done here."

Sarah held her stare on Gordon Williams a few more moments. To say anything would only lower herself to his level.

So instead she said, "Yes." And let Jack steer her away from the entrance of the village hall, back to meet up with her family.

The comedy or, in this case the tragedy, had indeed ended.

EPILOGUE

SETTING SUN IN her eyes, Sarah heard a slight whirr and turned to see Jack's fishing rod bend, as the line began feeding out from the reel.

"Got something?" she said.

"Appears so. Thought maybe I had gotten the whole fly thing wrong."

"Guess not."

She watched Jack begin to reel in the line very slowly, which is how she imagined such things were done. Her own father had been uninterested in such pastimes.

But she made a mental note: take the children fishing sometime, before they're all grown and that window shuts for ever.

Then — a splash a few yards away from the boat as the fish flew out of the water.

Sarah leaned forward. "Fantastic. Never seen that."

Jack kept reeling.

"Not the biggest trout I've ever seen. But should make a nice meal."

The trout jumped one more time, twisting and turning, catching the sunlight.

"Grab the net if you would."

Sarah grabbed the long pole, and leaned close to the edge.

MURDER ON THAMES

"Now, when you can see him beside the boat, just scoop in and pull him out."

The fish kept twisting in the water, but it didn't jump again, and when it was nearly below her, Sarah leaned out, dipped the net into the water, and snagged the fish.

Jack had a big grin as Sarah held out his trophy to him.

"Well done," she said.

"Dinner!" he said. "And I do believe it's martini time."

JACK HAD ICY martinis in classic glasses in their hands in minutes.

"Stay for the fish?" he asked. "Doesn't get any fresher."

Sarah smiled. "I'd love to. But I need to get back for the children, they'll be wanting a proper home-cooked meal tonight. Much as I can cook. Which isn't much."

Jack brought his martini glass close and clinked with Sarah.

"Here's to your detective work."

"Here's to *our* detective work."

"Always feels good. This solving mysteries thing."

"Yes. Kind of... exciting."

He turned to her. "And you know your friend Alan? He even said 'thanks'. Got the feeling that he doesn't mind quite as much having an old NYPD pro like me on the home — what do you call it?"

"Turf?"

"Yes. And now we know that your sweet old Cherringham may not be so cosy and innocent, who knows? There may be more ahead."

She hadn't even thought about that. She had done this for Sammi. But it had been better than fun.

Exciting, challenging — and Jack? Well Jack was Jack. Who

wouldn't want to play detective with the best?

"Sure. So," she said, "Here's to more."

"Yes. Just as long as it's not tonight. I have, as they say, a fish to fry."

Then they both turned back to the setting sun, for a last quiet sip of the icy drink.

As Sarah knew that life in Cherringham — for both of them — had suddenly become much more interesting.

NEXT IN THE SERIES:

CHERRINGHAM

A COSY CRIME SERIES

MYSTERY AT THE MANOR

Matthew Costello & Neil Richards

The elderly owner of Mogdon Manor, Victor Hamblyn, dies in a mysterious fire. But was it really an accident? Jack and Sarah are sceptical... The victim's three middle-aged children, who all live in the village of Cherringham, are possible heirs. And possible murderers... Did one of them set the fire?

ABOUT THE AUTHORS

Matthew Costello (US-based) and **Neil Richards** (UK) have been writing TV scripts together for more than twenty years. The best-selling Cherringham series is their first collaboration as fiction writers: since its first publication as ebooks and audiobooks the series has sold over a million copies.

Matthew is the author of many successful novels, including *Vacation* (2011), *Home* (2014) and *Beneath Still Waters* (1989), which was adapted by Lionsgate as a major motion picture. He has written for The Disney Channel, BBC, SyFy and has also written dozens of bestselling games including the critically acclaimed *The 7th Guest*, *Doom 3*, *Rage* and *Pirates of the Caribbean*.

Neil has worked as a producer and writer in TV and film, creating scripts for BBC, Disney, and Channel 4, and earning numerous Bafta nominations along the way. He's also written script and story for over 20 video games including *The Da Vinci Code* and *Broken Sword*.

Made in the USA
Middletown, DE
24 August 2023

37300385R00076